A CRIME CLUB SELECTION

DON CADEE, Chief of Store Protection at Ambletts—swank Fifth Avenue department store—had seen triangles before. But this one had angles he couldn't figure at all.

Why had wealthy restaurateur Peter Baskoulos refused to pay for his wife's $9000 purchase of menswear? Why was Mrs. Baskoulos, a striking blonde, described by the clerk as "dark, like a gypsy"? And why did an eager young stockroom boy suddenly disappear?

Don had only a few leads to work with. But murder, a vicious beating, and a strange group of fortunetellers were leads he would rather have left unchecked . . .

Scene: New York City

This novel has not appeared in any form prior to book publication.

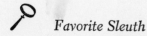

Favorite Sleuth

Books by SPENCER DEAN

THE MERCHANT OF MURDER
DISHONOR AMONG THIEVES
MURDER ON DELIVERY
MARKED DOWN FOR MURDER
THE FRIGHTENED FINGERS
THE SCENT OF FEAR

THE
MERCHANT
OF
MURDER

SPENCER DEAN

Published for the Crime Club by
DOUBLEDAY & COMPANY, INC.
Garden City, New York
1959

All of the characters in this book are fictitious,
and any resemblance to actual persons, living or dead,
is purely coincidental.

Library of Congress Catalog Card Number 59-6263

Copyright © 1959 by Doubleday & Company, Inc.
All Rights Reserved
Printed in the United States of America
First Edition

THE MERCHANT OF MURDER

THE MERCHANT OF MURDER

Nothing to be afraid of——

THE WOMAN walked rapidly past the store, scarcely turning her head as she glanced within. There didn't seem to be anyone inside, but she was sure that lustrous black eyes would be watching her from some slit in that curtain of rust-red carpets spread along the saggy clothesline at the rear.

Probably it would be safe to go in, now . . . but first she would walk to the corner and back, to give her heart time to stop its hammering. Or more truthfully, time to postpone the dreaded moment of decision, even if only for a few minutes—though actually the decision had already been made and it was already too late to turn back.

The bright April sun accentuated the tawdriness of the littered tenement hallways, shone pitilessly on the wretched junk in the secondhand shops. The air, which had seemed so sparkling and springlike on Park Avenue, was now tainted by sour smells of cabbage, odors from the dingy little fish market.

A gangly youth in a green satin jacket, which reached nearly to the knees of his peg-top pants, flipped a languid hand from his lounging post by the door of a cobbler's shop:

"Hey, baby! Maybe?"

She swung about, hurried back toward the store with the curious sign in the window. It was not so much that she was alarmed by the vulgarity; wolf whistles—and often the whistlers—had followed her ever since she had swaggered down

9

Jerome Avenue in her first jaunty sweater and buttock-tight blue jeans. Even now, after ten years, she did not have to examine her strawberry-and-cream complexion in the mirror to be certain that she still attracted a special sort of male attention. Though these days it would be in the lobby of the Pierre or the lounge at the Meadowbrook instead of at the fountain in some Bronx drugstore. But smug juvenile satisfaction at being able to arouse such obvious approaches had long since turned into mildly irritable resentment.

Nor did she entertain any illusion that her exquisitely plain Carnegie suit or her extravagantly simple Molyneux cloche was responsible for that staccato of metal heelplates on the sidewalk behind her now. It wasn't her full-blown figure or her bisque doll face which was luring that predatory youth; it was her ostrich-leather handbag, she was sure. How horrible it would be if that bag should be snatched away from her at the last instant——

She ran the last few steps, flung open the door so abruptly that the cardboard sign of the zodiac was torn from its thumb-tacked mooring. Once inside, she slammed the door behind her, stood with her back to it, panting.

The layers of overlapping oriental rugs, hung across the rear of the almost empty store, parted quickly to allow a slender girl to emerge with a curiously sensuous, almost sinuous glide. She was, perhaps, twenty; the stolidity of her handsome face was heightened by her wooden-Indian coloration. Her skin was the shade of weathered and varnished oak; her smooth hair, drawn back tightly from her forehead into a bun at the nape of her neck, might have been a wig hammered out of dull copper. The cigar-store-Indian effect was increased by a basilisk stare from dark, lustrous eyes like bits of black glass glinting in the afternoon sunshine. Yet there was nothing menacing about her voice; it was husky and softly sympathetic.

"You are afraid, dear."

"A man was following me."

"He will not follow you in here, you know that." The girl smoothed her gold-embroidered, black, toga-like robe, thoughtfully. "Still you are afraid."

"Not any more." The woman turned to peer through the flyspecked window. The green satin jacket was not in sight. "I'm all right, now."

"Did you make up your mind, dear?"

"Oh, yes. Yes, I have." The woman opened her bag. "I . . . I have it, in here."

"All of it?" The black eyes did not look at the handbag; the husky voice seemed almost disinterested.

"Yes, oh yes. Every . . . last penny." The answer came a trifle too readily.

"Then there is nothing to be afraid of, dear." The black-robed figure glided to the tent-front opening in the rust-red curtains, reappeared with a brass tripod some three feet high, from which depended, on an iron chain, a brass bowl the size of a basketball. "If you are still sure you want me to help you, I will do my best to cast out all fear from your heart."

"I'm very sure." The woman reached into the bag, brought out a packet of greenbacks folded once, bound with an elastic band. The bundle of bills was about three inches thick; the figure on the topmost bill was 500. She held out the packet. "Here."

"Oh no. No. I don't want to touch it." The basilisk eyes ignored the packet. "I told you. I don't want to have anything to do with it." A sharper tone came into the soft voice. "That is evil money. We have found that out. It would bring sorrow and grief to anyone who touched it. It would weigh down any living soul with its burden of betrayal, dear." The girl lit a match, dropped it in the brass bowl. Flames flickered up in the sunlight like small gilt tongues. "I cannot take your burden from you. You must do it for yourself."

11

"Yes." Suddenly, looking at the dancing flames, the woman felt suffocated. "I will."

"You must not be afraid, then." The girl produced a large, soiled red bandanna, stooped to spread it on the floor beside the tripod. "You are afraid no longer?"

"No." Did the monosyllable give her away with some uncontrollable quiver? Of course she was afraid. She would not have entered this dirty little store at all, day before yesterday, if she had not been almost out of her mind with fear. Fear multiplied many times because it was not for herself alone, fear compounded because there had been absolutely no one she could turn to for advice. Until she had found that strange bit of pasteboard—*Priestess of Peace of Mind*—there had not been one living soul in whom she would have dared to confide. Nor had her first sight of this grubby place with its queer musty smell, its two tattered canvas yacht chairs and its cabalistic charts hung on the scabrous walls been in the least reassuring.

Yet this girl had been so . . . so perceptive. No one could possibly have known of the secret plan to come down to this poverty-stricken section. The woman had made the trip downtown without much hope. She knew fortune tellers were usually frauds who made predictions which were calculated to flatter and fool one. But this girl with the brooding glance and the soothing voice had been different from all expectations, had said nothing about the future but instead had confined herself to the woman's past. Surely there was reason to believe in someone who knew so much after asking no more than a dozen questions about her birth date, her wedding date, her parents' death dates. How could one help but believe in Peace-of-Mind when its Priestess had been able to tell all about the woman she had never seen before, had even plucked out of the flames in that brass bowl the woman's name . . . and the name, too, of the man!

"Put the evil thing on that." The gypsy motioned toward the bandanna. "Then we will kneel and pray." She dropped gracefully to one knee.

The woman knelt on the hard planking, dropped the wad of money on the kerchief.

"First you must tie it up, dear. The opposite corners, tie them tightly. You must do all this yourself or it will come to no good."

The woman set her bag against the carpet-drapery to make a bandanna bundle.

"*Marbola ghanza,*" muttered the Priestess. "Whatever harm is in this thing, let it now be forever destroyed. Whatever hurt was in the heart, let it now be eased for all eternity. Whatever hate burned in the brain, let it now be burned to nothing." She picked up the bundle by one of its red-figured ears, held it over the flames. "Say it after me, dear. Whatever harm . . ."

". . . is in this thing . . ."

". . . let it be forever destroyed." The bandanna fell into the blazing bowl.

"Let it be—oh!" The woman gasped, rocked back on her heels, as a puff of dense white smoke burst from the brazier.

"Whatever hurt was in the heart . . ." intoned the gypsy.

". . . was in the heart." The woman felt her pulse pounding like a runaway horse as she watched flames rise high above the brass rim of the bowl. "Ah!" she recoiled again as a wild moan came from the tripod. She clutched the gypsy's arm. "*What was that?*"

"The devil in that money, dying." The Priestess, herself, seemed startled. "We are killing the evil, dear. But we must not stop. Repeat after me— 'Whatever hate burned in the brain . . .'" She passed her hand over the tripod as an incantation.

". . . whatever hate burned—*oh, my God!*"

13

The moan rose to a hideous shriek. Smoke billowing from the bowl became suddenly a lurid red, shot through with roiling black fumes.

"*Finish—finish!*" the gypsy cried. "Let it now be burned to nothing." She fell forward, her head bumping against the floor with a thud.

". . . burned to nothing." Sweat glistened on the woman's face; she could scarcely make out her own faint voice.

"We have done it." The gypsy writhed as if in agony. "It was a dangerous thing to do, but it is done. And now there is nothing to be afraid of, ever. Except——" She came to her knees.

"Except . . . *what?*"

"Except of . . . anyone finding out about what we have done." The Priestess sprang to her feet, eyes bright with apprehension. "You must swear on the things you hold most holy that you will never reveal to anyone what has happened here."

"I . . . I swear it." The woman stumbled against the wall, pushed herself erect.

"If you do, all the evil will come back a thousandfold. Your heart will rot away within you! Your brain will melt in burning torment!"

"I'll never breathe a word."

"Then go now. Go straight home. Lie down for an hour. Sleep, sleep with no fear of anything. And when you wake, the devil that has tortured you so long will have disappeared, forever. Go now, quickly—for I am exhausted."

"But——" The woman reached down for her bag.

"No, no! Go! Go! You owe me nothing. Nothing." The gypsy slithered through the slit in the carpeting.

The woman staggered out to the street, blinking dazedly at the sunshine.

I

LEAD-GRAY CLOUDS hung threateningly close above the stone-gray austerity of Ambletts that Tuesday after Easter. From across the Hudson, thunder grumbled at noontime crowds window-worshiping at Gotham's first temple of fashion.

Behind the block-long expanse of plate glass, the traditional *décor* of chick yellow and Easter-egg lavender had been succeeded by a more *soigné* display of June debwear arrayed on frozen-faced mannequins posturing in improbable imitation of the snooty set, at the country club, at any Ivy League prom, at a coming-out party in the Starlight Room.

But if it was already summer on the street, it was still springtime within the Store Superlative. Gay colors splashed the counters, bright bunches of flowers illuminated chaste showings of silverware, the fragrance of blossoms drifted pleasantly along the wide aisles. Signs of spring were everywhere—even in the office of the Chief of Store Protection.

One was the narrow shaft of sunshine dancing in the western window, enameling with glowing yellow a vaseful of jonquils on Don Cadee's desk, putting a touch of gilt on his prematurely white hair. Another was the April-on-the-boulevards effect of Sibyl Forde's periwinkle suit, the sweet-William-haloed bonnet, the choker of real narcissus. She perched on the corner of the desk, displaying nylons rather more agreeably than they were presented at Hosiery, Section Four.

"A new twist every day." He admired the legs but transferred his attention quickly to the choker. "Used to be you could only do three things with a flower like that—make a bouquet for the church, stick a few in a vase in the living room, or pin one on your lapel. But that arrangement is becoming." A cabbage leaf, he thought, would have been attractive on the girl with the perky, upturned nose, the radiant smile, the disconcerting green eyes.

"It's pretty," she agreed, "but impractical when worn in wrestling bouts."

"Did you make a grab?"

"Just wrestled a wench upstairs from Handkerchiefs. Speaking of new twists, she has one, too. She wears gloves at work."

He was astonished; it was an unwritten law of the light-fingered sorority that they conducted their pilfering bare-handed. "What were they? Thin silk?"

"Thick kid. Expensive imports. She probably stole those, too. I haven't checked with Gloves, yet. But they stood out like sore thumbs on her because her suit was strictly off the pipe racks, one flight up."

"An old pro?"

"A slick amateur, Don. I never could actually catch her tucking those five-dollar Zurich handkerchiefs inside her left glove, but one second they'd be in plain sight, then alla-gazam, the disappearing act. Time I caught on, she had five of those wispy goodies stuffed into her grubby little palm."

He smiled—partly to express his approval of the 'grab' but mainly to conceal his disappointment at not being able to take ten minutes from store business to discuss their personal plans for the week end—a matter of a drive up to a cottage which was for sale on a not-too-accessible lake in Connecticut, a transaction looking ahead to the time when she would be

16

more than his best operative. "We better nip that technique in the bud before she teaches it to a whole bevy of boosters." He rose; before he could move around his desk the ruby eye of the intercom winked. He flicked the switch. "Yes, Becky?"

His secretary's voice came through with a puzzled intonation. "Mister Stolz wants to see you right away; he's in a swivet. And Mister Martin says he has to see you immedjut, too. He's in a dither."

"Get the Credit Department, first." He reached for his phone; it buzzed immediately. "Mister Martin? Bill . . . this is Don."

"Oh, brother. You heard from Bob Stolz?"

"He just sent for me. Is he blowing up a storm?"

"The cyclone warnings are out."

"What's the twist on the twister?"

"Peter Baskoulos is in his office. *The* Mister B."

"One who runs that chain of restaurants?"

"That's the fellow. He runs an open account with us, too—any amount of credit. Never had any difficulty with him, payment on the nose every tenth. Until today." The Credit Manager was evidently under a strain. "We have a special arrangement with him—we mail a duplicate of all bills directly to his office the day after the purchases are made. Maybe he wants to keep tabs on the way his wife is spending money."

"For a man who races a big stable of thoroughbreds and owns a two-hundred-foot yacht, it seems a cautious procedure," Don said. "But if he always okays her bills——"

"He's not okaying one we sent out yesterday for twenty-one hundred and thirty some dollars. Seems she came in Saturday, ran hog-wild in Menswear—nylon shorts by the dozen, silk shirts in twenty patterns, cashmere socks in eight pastel shades, enough pajamas to——"

"What's the complaint? Doesn't he like his wife to pick out his shirts?"

17

"She's never bought anything but neckties for him; she doesn't even know what size shorts he wears. He has all his shirts made to order, anyhow."

"Oh! So?"

"So not only is he refusing to honor the charge but now he's bellowing for affidavits from Ambletts to support a suit for divorce!"

"Hm . . ."

"Thing that puts us in the middle, his wife denies having been in the store at all on Saturday. Says she never bought underwear for any man in her whole life."

"Well, there's actually nothing reprehensible about it . . . still, it might be construed as suggestive under certain circumstances." The intercom button glowed, went out, glowed again twice in rapid succession. "Hold everything, Bill. Get back to you as soon as I've seen the boss." Don hung up. "Sib, have one of the other operatives question your glove-fingered amateur. Want you to hop right down to Menswear, find out who sold a slew of stuff to Peter Baskoulos' wife last Saturday."

Sibyl slid off the desk. "Was there some hitch in the transaction?"

"He seems to believe his fair lady has been buying shorts and so on for some joy friend."

"Oh no." The green eyes narrowed; she frowned. "Missus Baskoulos was Rina Ardoni, the dancer. She's been around Broadway too long to try anything as stupid as that. She'd never have been silly enough to have presents of that sort charged."

"Not unless she was scheming to leave Baskoulos' bed and board; I agree. Something fishy going on; dig up those details downstairs."

On the way up in the Executive elevator, he considered possible explanations. It might have been some other charge

18

customer who had bought the merchandise; mistakes in billing *were* made, sometimes, even at Ambletts. Or Mrs. Peter Baskoulos might have gone off her rocker, temporarily, bought a lot of things for which she had no earthly use and was now too ashamed to admit the purchases. That sort of thing did occasionally happen.

The only other alternative seemed to be that someone had impersonated the restaurant magnate's wife, had somehow managed to have a couple of thousand dollars' worth of merchandise charged to Baskoulos' account. That was the kind of slip-up against which Ambletts was supposed to have a foolproof system of safeguards—carefully registered credit coins, personal identification required by the Section Manager on all purchases exceeding one hundred dollars, lacking which, telephoned confirmation from the customer's bank. And surely, the wholesale amounts of merchandise should have warned Menswear to be more than ordinarily cautious.

Don had never seen the man who had parlayed a Greek quick-lunch counter into a gastronomical fortune, but had mentally pictured the man as the little Napoleon type, short, dark, dynamic. But the straddle-legged individual jutting a belligerent chin at Bob Stolz was tall, broad-shouldered, handsome; the owner of the Restaurant Grand Luxe chain might have been an Ivy League fullback, a score of years out of college. He did have the curly black hair and bristling brows of his Grecian forebears; the anger in the glowering gray eyes might have been the rage of one used to having his tyrannical moods humored.

Bob Stolz was relieved to have help in handling the man; the General Manager's tomato-ruddy features relaxed as he made the introduction. "Pete, this is Don Cadee; he has a rep for straightening out mix-ups of this sort with complete discretion."

"Hell with discretion," growled Baskoulos. "If you people think you can cover up for Rina, you're off on the wrong foot. I know she bought these items; I know who she bought 'em for. All I want from you is a sworn statement that'll stand up in court."

Don took the bull by the horns. "You have the reputation, Mister Baskoulos, of being too good a businessman to pass hasty judgment before you have all the facts."

The big man waved an Ambletts' billhead under Don's nose. "I don't mind paying your damned bill; it'll save me alimony a hundred times over. But don't give me that 'facts' stuff; you sold her these shorts and undershirts, she took them with her, that half-pint jockey is probably wearing some of them right now. You get me that sworn statement or I'll sue you blue in the face."

"You're a gambling man," Don said evenly. "I'll make you a bet. The amount of that bill against the best dinner your restaurants can offer—that your wife never ordered a dollar's worth of that merchandise."

Baskoulos glared; tiny red veins showed on the whites of his eyes; his thick neck thrust forward. "I've a better proposition for you, Mister Cadee. If you're wrong, you pay Hayworth Greld's funeral expenses. Because I'm going to crack his neck with these two hands if I never see another sunrise." He took a sudden step forward; his hands came close to Don's throat.

Not since the banzai charges on Guadalcanal had Don seen the desire to kill so plain in any man's eyes.

II

FOR A moment Don thought the Greek was about to throttle him; the bloodshot eyes suggested that the muscular fingers would gladly go to work on Don if he attempted interference in this *affaire de coeur*.

Bob Stolz broke the tension with a "Take it easy, Pete," hurried to fling his arm around the big man's shoulder. "Simmer down, pardner."

The glare did not leave Baskoulos' eyes, the killer expression remained as unchanged as if the savage scowl had been chiseled onto the stony face, but Zeus descended, reluctantly, from the Olympian heights of his rage. All he said was "Don't cross me up, Cadee, fair warning."

Don didn't answer him. "Bob . . . I'll get back to you in fifteen minutes." When he closed the door of the sanctum, the General Manager was saying something to Baskoulos about a tranquilizer.

Maybe, Don thought, he'd gone too far out on the limb. If it turned out he'd made a sour guess, he might get this jockey Greld backed up in a coffin corner. And he would sure as hell get himself a black mark in Bob Stolz's book, if he had miscalled the turn of the card.

The aisles in Menswear were swarming with lunch-hour shoppers, mostly women. The nylon boxer counter was two-deep; mink stoles and Skye tweeds were clustered around the Basque shirt Special. Sibyl Forde stood at the Section Wrapping Desk talking to a redheaded boy in a dun-colored jacket with *Stock Room* stitched across the upper right sleeve. Her nephew—the boy Don had gone to bat for a couple of months ago, to help him land the job.

Sibyl caught sight of Don, touched her clenched fist lightly to the boy's chin, dismissing him. "Frank Wilmar's out for lunch, Don. But Lois Anderson, the salesgirl, says there couldn't have been any possibility of a mistake."

"I'd say there were several, Sib." Don ruffled the rusty thatch amiably; the boy grinned. "One was to let a couple of thousand bucks' worth of merchandise walk out on two legs. Aside from Furs, name one department where a sale of that size is a take-home transaction."

"Jewelry, perhaps. But you are right," she admitted, "though in this case there was some reason for the rush-and-carry. Lois says the things were to be a surprise for Mister Baskoulos just before they went abroad on a wedding anniversary trip."

"The gentleman didn't mention any such excursion," Don said. "Besides, it's not usual for transatlantic trippers to load up on wearing apparel before going to Europe; generally they wait to get on the other side before they start on a spending spree."

Timmy Forde exclaimed, "It sure was a spree, Mister Cadee. That chauffeur had to make four trips out to the car."

"Tim." Sibyl tweaked the lobe of the boy's ear. "Tend to your own knitting."

The boy wrinkled his nose at her, moved away with a parting shot: "All right, but I told you: I thought at the time there was something funny about that chauffeur of hers. His fingernails were dirty."

Don followed the stock boy with thoughtful eyes. "If that

delinquent nephew of yours doesn't reform, he might wind up in a Store Protection office one of these days."

"He notices everything. Sometimes things which aren't really there." She caught his arm, pulled him toward a sporty display of wool Argyles. "Lois is making out a sales slip; she'll be free in a minute."

The salesgirl was the slender, pallid variety with bony shoulders and a neck that was a little too long, a bit too thin. She looked as if a month on an Arizona dude ranch would do her a world of good. She was understandably nervous as Sibyl beckoned her away from the sock counter.

"Tell Mister Cadee what you told me about Missus Baskoulos, Lois."

"I'm so flustered . . . I hope I can remember . . . it was the biggest book I've made in the three years I've been here." The Anderson girl fussed with a coltish mane. "It simply never occurred to me there might be anything wrong with the sale, Mister Cadee. She looked like a million dollars . . . and when she opened her bag to get out her coin, it looked to me as if she had pretty near a million in the roll that was in there . . . I'd never seen a five-hundred bill before."

Don said: "She didn't have her money in a wallet, Lois?"

"No, sir. She had her wallet in there . . . she showed it to Mister Wilmar, with her driver's license and her credit cards . . . but all this money was in a big fat roll with an elastic band around it."

"Tell him," Sibyl urged, "how she was dressed."

"Well, she wore this nifty beige suit . . . I think it's the color they call Bahama Sand . . . I *believe* it was custom tailored, though of course I can't be sure. She had a figure that would make even a cheap suit look good."

Sibyl said: "You mentioned something about her haughty manner."

"Maybe that was just my imagination." A harried expression came into the salesgirl's eyes. "When she began to discard anything but the most expensive numbers and after she started to order those eight-dollar cashmere socks by the dozen, I suppose I got it into my head that she was used to nothing but the best and then, every time I showed her something like those Italian silk pajamas— 'Don't you have anything better, dear?'—so maybe the idea of her being snobbish just built up in my mind. She kept me so busy, showing her everything new and ordering right and left—and I was so excited, thinking what a terrific book I'd have for the week— I guess I got a little rattled. I'm sorry I can't be of more help."

"You've been a big help, Lois." Don patted a thin shoulder reassuringly. "Not a thing for you to fret about."

"Hope you're right, Don." A short, plump man with thinning hair and sharp brown eyes behind gold-rimmed spectacles came up beside Sibyl. "Bill tells me there's some trouble about that Baskoulos windfall."

Sibyl linked an arm into Frank Wilmar's. "We know you took all the precautions."

Don said: "Sure her coin was genuine, Frank?"

"Take my oath on it. I'm too old at this business to be fooled by a fake." But the Section Manager seemed distraught. "Besides, the lady didn't wait for me to run through the routine, she came to me from Ida Lanning in Lingerie— her chauffeur had the packages with him—and said Miss Lanning had been good enough to recommend me to assist her in making some selections for her husband. I said I'd be delighted—when she showed me her identification cards and her Ambletts' credit coin and I realized who she was, I *was* delighted."

"You'd never seen her before?" Don asked.

"Not actually. Pictures of her in the newspapers, but I wouldn't be able to recognize my best friend from some of those pictures. Still everyone knows her husband is a multi-

multi and I had read about her often enough; I knew Missus Baskoulos was Italian and this lady had a dark complexion, like so many Italians. Naturally I didn't want to seem to doubt an important customer; however, there was that rule about telephoned verification in case of personal unfamiliarity with the purchaser. But she didn't wait for me on that, either."

"She saved you the trouble," Don made it a flat statement, "by calling up herself?"

"Oh no. No indeed." Wilmar shook his head so his spectacles glittered. "I know that dodge. She said she wanted to ask her husband's secretary about sizes on certain garments; would I be kind enough to call his office and say that Missus Baskoulos wanted a word with the secretary."

Don felt like smiling, but refrained. "She gave you the phone number?"

"Yes. But it was Baskoulos' office, right enough. The girl who answered said 'Grand Luxe Corporation' in that sing-song way the operators have."

"And then," Don said, "the lady spoke to the secretary?"

"In Greek. Or maybe it was Italian. Some foreign language." Wilmar fidgeted with his spectacles, took them off, twirled them by the earpiece.

Lois said: "I heard her; of course I couldn't understand what she was saying but I heard her mention 'Peter' several times."

"She talked," the Section Manager added defensively, "quite a long time. Three or four minutes, at least."

Don sighed. That made it all right. She didn't hang up right away on the party at the other end of the line. That was a guarantee of her identity—that she spoke to someone at a number she gave! He went behind the Argyle counter to the interdepartmental phone.

The trio watched anxiously as he dialed. The Section Manager, peering nearsightedly, his forehead corrugated like

25

a toy washboard. The apprehensive salesgirl, chewing on a little-finger nail. And Sibyl with puzzled eyes, studying Wilmar.

"Lingerie? Miss Lanning? Ida? . . . Don Cadee . . . that's right, still after the malefactors of great stealth. One, especially, who seems to have been in your Section last Saturday. Missus Peter Baskoulos. Claimed you sent her to Frank Wilmar in Menswear . . . no? . . . no recollection of her at all? . . . you never did send any customer to Frank? . . . thanks a lot, Ida."

Frank Wilmar's fingers shook as he put on his spectacles. "I can't believe it, Don. She seemed so . . . legitimate."

"She took pains with her masquerade." Don seemed to be excusing those who had been taken in. "I expect we'll have to take considerable pains if we're going to trace her."

"Oh!" Lois said, "I feel just miserable about it."

Sibyl comforted her. "With her identification cards and the coin, anyone might have been tricked into believing her."

"Sure." The matter of Ambletts' coin bothered Don, too, but he was careful not to show it. "Can either of you recall anything else about the lady? Birthmarks or skin blemishes?"

"Her skin," the Section Manager stated heavily, "was smooth as satin. Dark, like—well, possibly more like an Indian than an Italian."

Sibyl asked: "Was she wearing rings? A wristwatch? A brooch or a pin?"

Lois said, "I can't remember——"

"She had a necklace." It was Timmy, behind a dolly loaded with boxes of belts and suspenders. "A queer old thing, made of gold coins strung on a gold chain, but they weren't American coins, I mean not United States gold pieces . . . they had some funny foreign faces on them."

Sibyl seized her nephew's arm, shook him. "Timmy Forde, you're just making it up."

26

"No, he isn't," cried Lois. "I recall it now. Just as he says, foreign money on a gold chain. Timmy's exactly right."

Don dialed once more. Dark-skinned like an Indian. Gold coins for a necklace. Bills in a roll like a gambler at a race track. A brazen impersonation. What more do you want!

"Charlotte, this is Don. Bob still there? With the bull of Bashan? Oh, he's rampaged away . . . well, let me talk to the boss . . . Bob? You know Mister Baskoulos pretty well?"

The General Manager said: "Sit on a couple Boards of Directors with him. Shoot eighteen holes with him, every now and then. But I've never seen him as wild as he was today."

"Know this wife of his, too?"

"Say I do."

"Is she dark-skinned, like a gypsy?"

"Hell, she's a ravishing blonde!"

"Then you can tell your pal Pete that he has no grounds of jealousy—so far as that merchandise is concerned, anyhow."

"Positive?"

"Absolutely. And equally sure that Ambletts has been rooked out of two thousand odd dollars' worth of merchandise, by the aforesaid gypsy sweetheart."

Over the profanity-punctured questions of Bob Stolz, Don could hear the piping voice of Timmy Forde:

"That's what she was, a gypsy! Surest thing you know—and you know what, Sibyl? There's a reward for the return of that merchandise. Guess who's going to get that reward!"

III

WEDNESDAY, TOO, was gray; ashen clouds were piled low across the Manhattan sky; gun-metal pools glistened on the Avenue; from Don's office window the wet sidewalks looked as if they might have been paved with raw oysters. The only bright note was Sibyl's gentian suit—but she herself was definitely not on the cheery side.

To begin with, she had been late, which was extraordinary, for she always made it a practice to range the aisles during the half hour between eight-thirty and nine to familiarize herself with such "specialties du jour" as the Store Superlative allowed itself to display. Then, she had not telephoned an explanation of her tardiness. Finally she had marched grimly into the office of the Chief of Store Protection at nine-fifteen with the brief announcement:

"Timmy's been out all night."

Don said: "Not home yet?"

"No. He went home for supper last night, told Edith he was going to find a gypsy woman who had swindled Ambletts; he was sure he could horn in on that reward the bonding company posted for fifty per cent of the value of the merchandise. That's the last she's heard from him."

"Maybe he came straight to the store this morning."

"I just checked with the stock room, Don. He's not on the

job; I have to phone Edith and tell her; she's just about out of her mind already."

He went to her quickly, put his arm around her. "And so are you, naturally."

"If anything has happened to him it would just about break my heart, Don. And it would literally kill Edith."

"This isn't the first time he's worried his mother by a stunt like this, Sib; you told me about a couple of his escapades."

"He ran away from home a couple of times, but that was when he was six or seven."

"You can't exactly call him grown up even now."

"Of course not. But he has *some* sense of responsibility— and he promised Edith he wouldn't stay out late. I'm scared something's happened to him, Don." There were no tears, but her tone said they were being held in check.

"That Timmy's a thoughtless brat," he consoled her. "But he's quite a lad. He may have stuck his neck out too far, but I expect he'll be able to pull his chin back in before anybody clouts it very hard."

"It won't make Edith feel any better to tell her that."

"No. Tell her to sit tight while we put the machinery in motion to look for him."

"The Missing Persons Bureau?"

"Maybe, later. You know their routine; they will start checking the hospitals and the morgue; they'll ring her up to get the names and addresses of Timmy's friends; before lunch time she would be in a panic."

"She's close to it, now."

"Sure. So tell her I'm already working on an angle that may turn up some news of him shortly."

"Can I tell her what it is?"

"Not yet; she might gum the works. I'm going up to see Missus Peter Baskoulos."

"What can she know about Timmy?"

29

"That gypsy had her credit coin, Sib. Baskoulos told Bob Stolz last night that his wife had lost the coin; didn't know how or where. If that's so, I won't get anywhere. But I don't think it's so. If Missus B. knows the name of that woman who impersonated her, I think we'll be able to locate Timmy before long."

"If I hadn't seen you pull rabbits out of an empty hat before, I'd say you were simply stalling in the hope that Timmy will show up, sooner or later."

"No parlor magic," he said soberly. "Nothing up either sleeve, except the fact that Missus B. didn't notify the store about the coin. That makes her liable for our loss; she knows it. It may be enough of a lever to pry out the name of the gypsy." He let her help him into his topcoat. "Meantime, you have another angle to work."

"The other stores?" she guessed.

"Find out who else she took, what she took 'em for, whether she used that same telephone dodge. Someone may remember the number. That might be a key."

"Who'll take over on the First?"

"I'll send Andy Ryan down there. See you at noon."

He walked up to the Baskoulos' apartment building, thinking about Timmy Forde every step of the way. Maybe the boy's mother should have been warned about the danger of letting the youngster go out, on his own, to hunt down a swindler—a band of swindlers, possibly, since the "chauffeur" had obviously been one of her gang. But Don had been too intent on straightening out Peter Baskoulos, had supposed Hayworth Greld had been the one in danger. So now Sibyl's nephew was . . . what? Too preoccupied with running down a swindler to give a thought to his mother and her sister-in-law? Or lying in some dark alley? Floating in the oily swirls of the East River?

Don was in no frame of mind to be put off with polite

evasions when he stopped at the twentieth floor where Peter Baskoulos had his river-view apartment. A maid in a fluffy-ruffle uniform turned up a sharply pointed nose on learning that he had no appointment:

"I will take in your name; you wait, please."

"No." He was brusque. "I can't wait. My business is urgent. Tell Missus Baskoulos that unless she prefers to have me go to Mister Baskoulos' office, she will have to talk to me right away."

The maid sniffed haughtily. She lifted her chin, looked down her nose disapprovingly. But she let him into a foyer the size of an ordinary living room, presently ushered him into a drawing room large enough to accommodate a sizable convention.

There was an immense fireplace, a gigantic U-shaped divan in white damask, a table topped with a slab of Carrara bigger than the dancing space in many a night club, a handsome break front into the lower part of which was built a collection of radio, television tubes, high-fidelity set, record cabinets. Whatever the lady's tastes might be, he decided, money was evidently no hindrance to her full enjoyment of them.

But he saw at once that she had style, at least, plus a shyly attractive personality. She had the grace of the professional dancer and the poise of the celebrity who has ceased to hold the center of the stage but has retained her in-the-spotlight manner. Yet he thought that beneath the assurance there was apprehension.

"You are from Ambletts." She indicated an armchair in scarlet leather, went on without waiting for him to sit. "I'm afraid I have acted very stupidly about the loss of my credit coin, Mister Cadee."

He nodded. "You may be able to repair some of the damage if you can tell me, now, where you"—he hesitated pointedly—"lost the coin."

31

"Why, of course," she agreed. "I would have done so Saturday, right after it happened, except that I was sure Peter would be furious with me. Because, you see, the coin was the least of it; I lost my handbag with a very large amount of cash in it . . . besides all my personal possessions, a ruby-studded compact, my driver's license, my keys—why, I was absolutely stunned at the time."

"There were other credit coins in the handbag?" he asked. "Coins from other department stores?"

"Oh yes, but it was the money which made me afraid to tell Peter. I had no business having that much cash with me, to begin with; I never do carry more than a couple of hundred, but I intended to buy a present for him and I couldn't pay for it by check because—well, it was a Degas he had always admired, the Picnic in the Park—perhaps you know the painting?"

"No."

"Well, it was up for auction at the Harker-Fenne Galleries, Saturday. I knew if I bid it in and paid by check the papers would run a story—'Show Girl Buys Old Master for Young Husband'—or some such trashy treatment. Anyway, I wanted to keep the purchase a secret until our anniversary, that's a couple of weeks from now. So I went to the bank and drew out all I had in my account, hoping I could bid in the painting without having to disclose my identity to the reporters—of course someone in the galleries might have recognized me, but there were a lot of other valuable items being offered and I thought I could get by without being noticed. But I made the mistake of stopping in at the Montalban—you know the Café Montalban?"

"Yes." One of those arty spots in the East Fifties where the Gray Flannel Suiters took their clients and the clients took their secretaries. "You went there for lunch?"

"A pick-me-up, really, to sustain me at the galleries. I'd

been there before, often. But this time, while I was freshening up in the powder room—I was utterly exhausted—all of a sudden I became aware that a woman who had followed me into the lavatory had whisked my handbag from the shelf above the basin and was slipping out the door."

He said nothing; he thought she was a trifle too unconcerned about how he was accepting her story.

"I dashed after her as soon as I recovered from my surprise, but she had quite a head start."

"Did you cry 'Stop, Thief' or call for help in catching her?"

"No. You see, I was so totally flabbergasted—I thought perhaps the woman might have taken my bag in mistake for her own. By the time I realized she was actually running away with all that cash, she was out on the street and I was making a perfect fool of myself, racing after her."

"How would you describe this woman?"

"She was dark, very dark, deep olive, I suppose you would say. Medium height, perhaps a little plump, it's so difficult to be sure, it all happened so quickly, and I was taken so completely by surprise. The first thing I knew, she was hopping into a car at the corner of East Fifty-sixth and Madison—and the car was pulling out into the northbound traffic."

"Did you look for a policeman?"

"Like a ninny, I fainted, blacked out as if someone had hit me on the head with a hammer."

"And when you came to?"

"There was a crowd around me—everyone making suggestions— 'Stand back, let her have some air'— 'Take her into the drugstore'— 'Call the cop, he'll get an ambulance'—you can imagine! My reluctance to having cheap publicity about buying the Degas was nothing compared to my fear of having it known that I had been robbed, that I was such a complete dumbskull, that I'd passed out on the street. Peter would have been a wild man if he had ever seen all that in the papers. So

I pulled myself together as best I could, mumbled my thanks, was helped into a taxi, and came directly home. Of course I simply did not have the courage to tell Peter what had happened. But I realize now that I should have notified your store; I'm terribly sorry."

"So am I," Don said. "Sorry to have to tell you that I don't believe a word of your story. I think you know the woman who took your bag and your money and our coin. I want the woman's name; I want to know where to find her."

Mrs. Baskoulos put on a good show of indignation. "You are insolent, young man. I am not used to having my word disbelieved. You mentioned to my maid that you might have to go to my husband if you did not talk to me. Well, you have spoken to me and now you may go and see Peter—who will very likely give you a hard time. Mitzi—Mister Cadee is leaving."

IV

HE HAD wanted to continue his interrogation, had had every intention of mentioning the missing teen-ager in order to pressure Mrs. Baskoulos into admitting the identity of the swindler. But the blonde had walked out on him; he couldn't very well follow her into her bedroom and apply third-degree methods. So he had departed from the Broadsworth apartment in a black mood.

The woman's story had been preposterous. The statements her husband had made in Bob Stolz's office the evening before were sufficient to establish the strained situation in the Baskoulos ménage; obviously she had not been about to spend all her available funds to buy an old masterpiece to present to him as a gesture of reconciliation.

Anyhow, if she had ever wished to make such a purchase in anonymity, nothing would have been easier than to get some art agent to act for her, to bid in the painting and deliver it to her later; that sort of thing was done all the time. The yarn about the need for lugging around a large sum of cash was completely incredible.

It was even more fantastic that she had expected him to believe that she would have allowed a thief to escape from the café without any outcry on her part. The tale about the mysterious car wouldn't have convinced a child. Mrs. Baskoulos hadn't noticed the mythical car's license number, hadn't even remarked on the make, model, or color of the getaway vehicle.

But however much of a fairy tale her recounting of the loss of the handbag had been, there had been nothing phony about her fear of her husband. So probably it wouldn't do any good to go to him and ask that he force her to tell the truth; she was clearly more afraid of his anger than of any consequences of her falsehood. Moreover, if she had reason to be so frightened of him, bringing out the facts might precipitate a family tragedy.

Yet some of the facts were as plain as the Greek's hot temper: the rich woman, the loss of a large amount of money, the possession of the credit coin—and hence also, in all likelihood the possession of the handbag—by a gypsy woman. A man would have to be without any sense of smell not to detect the odor of a confidence game.

Because of the boy Don had hoped to save time by short-cutting the prescribed routine—taking Frank Wilmar and the Anderson girl down to the Bureau of Identification at headquarters, having them look through the photos of gypsies who had run afoul of the law, hoping they could recognize the woman in the Bahama Sand suit. A fair percentage of local-resident gypsies would be represented in that catalogue of "mugged" persons—but the one who had put over the swindle was young; she might not have any record as yet. Or she might belong to one of the roving bands that hit New York only once every four or five years; there might be no picture of her anywhere. Yet it seemed the only chance.

There was no news of Timmy nor any word from Sibyl at the office when he got back. Becky Kahn had stacked a pile of paper work on his blotter: inventory loss reports from Leather Goods, Costume Jewelry, Lingerie, Cosmetics, Glassware—how come a shortage of six brandy snifters from Glassware? Had some booster sneaked those past a salesgirl by stuffing those fragile shells in a bag-skirt?—a long query from Ambletts' bonding company relative to the culpability of Menswear personnel in the Baskoulos business, a couple of signed Admission of Guilt cards from juvenile fountain-pen snatchers. He pushed the lot aside, called Stolz.

"Bob? Just back from talking to the ravishing blonde."

The General Manager fumed audibly. "Why in the hell can't you leave well enough alone, Don?"

"It's not well enough. One of our stock boys—the one who helped to spot that slicker as a gypsy—is missing; he went after the reward the bonding people offered for the arrest and conviction of store swindlers; he's been out all night and his mother is frantic."

Stolz grumbled. "You sound like a nervous old biddy yourself; since when have we been paying you to get up a sweat about every employee who doesn't show up for work!"

"He hasn't showed up for breakfast, Bob. And I am nervous. Kid is Timothy Forde, Sib's nephew."

"Now don't let your personal feelings——"

"——affect my professional attitude." Don finished it. "I know; I am. I have the feeling that boy's in trouble. That's why I went to see Missus B. First she told her husband she lost her handbag with our coin in it. Then she gave me the run-around with a wild recital of how the bag had been stolen. My belief is she was swindled out of the handbag and a big wad of bills by the same gypsy who walked out with our two thousand dollars' worth of Menswear."

"Hell, she's not hiring you to recover her property. And the bonding company's looking out for our interests . . ."

"They're not looking for the boy; that's what I am concerned about, Bob. If the kid managed to get a line on those

37

gypsies, and followed it up, Ambletts might have to send flowers. My notion was, the ravishing blonde could tell me where to locate that precious pair of swindlers. But she wouldn't."

"Godsake!" The grumble deepened with exasperation. "You're going off the deep end. You don't know the Forde youngster has been hurt or worse. You can't even be sure he isn't hitchhiking to California or that he hasn't signed on some cattle boat as cabin boy. You certainly wouldn't seriously claim that Rina Baskoulos would have a hand in harming the lad."

"Quite right on all counts, Bob. Still——"

"Still you want to put yourself in the middle of a family quarrel. You stay out of it, hear? That's an order. I happen to think that Peter's mistaken Rina's interest in his Old Plantation Stables for affection for that jockey. But, in any case, if there are going to be fireworks, you let someone else touch 'em off, understand?"

Don said he understood the General Manager's viewpoint and would be guided thereby. How far he would be guided by it he didn't specify. For the Cyclopean eye of the intercom and Becky's voice said Big Pat had a message for him: he listened while Stolz repeated his admonition, then hung up.

"Send Pat in, Becky."

The huge bulk of the uniformed guard at the First-floor escalator shouldered into the office. Pat seldom left his post by the moving stairway; it must have taken an emergency to bring him up to the Protection office, Don decided. He had a warm feeling for this hulking Hibernian who had given up pickpocketing on the afternoon Don had picked him up in Toys with a collection of "leathers" the big man hadn't been able to dispose of in time. How any heavyweight could be so light-fingered had always been a puzzle, but Pat had worked out very well with Ambletts, had justified Don's faith and confounded the bonding company, which had strongly opposed hiring him.

"What you got, Pat?"

"I was ast to hand this to you, personally, Mister Cadee." He held out a sealed envelope, wrapped with adhesive tape. In round, juvenile letters, it was addressed in pencil to Mister Donald Cadee, Chief, Protection, Ambletts, Fifth Avenue.

"Who gave it to you, Pat?"

"Girl, what the ads call a pre-teener. Runny nose skinnamarink, maybe ten, eleven. Looked like she come from one of those underprivileged homes, shoes all scuffed out, you know. I caught her sneakin' up the esc'lator, thought maybe she was a purse snatcher like that one I grabbed couple weeks ago. But no, she fights me; says she has a letter to deliver to you, personally. So, rather than raise a rumpus on the floor, I guarantee to her I will hand it to you direct, myself."

"Then you let her go?"

"She ran like a rabbit the minute I had the letter in my fist. Should I of held her?"

"No, it's all right. You handled it nicely. Thank you, Patrick."

When the outsize uniform had shouldered out, Don opened the envelope. The letter had been written on cheap, ruled notebook paper, the words spaced widely as if the writer had taken a good deal of time to think out just what to say:

Dear Mister Cadee,

I am in a bad jam about that mdse. on the Baskoulos order and I guess I should of minded my own business but I thought it was and did not mean to get anyone in trouble on acct. of it.

No one is making me write this letter, actually it is my own idea, but of course they will read it. So about all I can say now is that the certain party who got the mdse. was owed a lot of money by Mister Baskoulos and wouldn't pay it to her. So after all this time she took that means of getting even with him, which he could well afford. Anyway she has gotten rid of the mdse. already and no longer has it in her possession and will call the matter square if it is dropped.

I told them it was up to you, whether the store would proscute or not. If you give them your word not to, they will let me go home which I will be awful glad to do, because mom gets pretty upset if I am out even an hour after 12 oclock and here it is pretty near a whole day.

What they want you to do is call up this number, it's a bar and grill somewhere I don't know exactly where, but the number is Mulberry 9-7166 at five oclock this afternoon, on the dot, and ask for Mister Stryker, that's all. It wouldn't do any good to notify detectives or have the F B I in on it because there won't be any Mister Stryker there. But the bar tender will holler out and ask is Mister Stryker there and he won't be but someone will hear the question and pass along the word that you don't mean to proscute so I can go home.

Your friend,
Timothy J. Forde

Don was reading the letter for the second time when Becky's voice announced:

"Miss Forde, Mister Cadee."

V

SHE CAME in with her customary jaunty stride, but the perky smile was lacking:

"Any word?"

He shook his head, arranging the inventory loss reports over Timmy's letter. "You know what 'no news' is supposed to be."

"It's not good, no matter what they say. When you're waiting like this, it's gray hairs and nightmares and nervous breakdowns. Did your angle pay off?"

"Not so far. I learned the lady is a liar by the clock but I can't find out why she feels compelled to take up fairy tales at her age. I satisfied myself she knows this gypsy but I couldn't get her to admit it."

"Did you tell her about Timmy?"

"Never got the chance, Sib. She threw me out soon as I let her know I didn't buy her crazy, mixed-up explanation of the theft of her handbag."

She dropped dejectedly into the chair by the Avenue window. "We have to find that boy or Edith will lose her mind. There must be something we can do."

"There is. I'll take Frank Wilmar and Lois Anderson downtown on the Crook's Tour; they can run through the Rogues in a couple of hours. If they can't spot the gyp's portrait, maybe they will recognize that 'chauffeur' who attracted

Timmy's attention." He slid the boy's letter in the side pocket of his coat while she was gazing out of the window. "If you come up with any kind of solid description, we'll make a trip to the Bureau of Identification card files."

"What I gathered was a composograph; a sort of witches' brew with a little of everything in it."

"Does it check with Lois Anderson's picture of the witch?"

"It doesn't check with anything. She took three other stores with that toplofty act of hers; the best the store people could do was three differing sets of data. The fake Missus B. was tall, medium height or below average—take your choice. On her weight, the guesses run from one hundred sixty, short and chubby—one hundred thirty, medium and slim trim—one hundred ten, tall and bean pole-ish."

"A mite confusing when it comes to sending out a flyer on her."

"Only thing all three stores agree on is her coloration but one thought she was a Brahmin, one a Portugee, and one an oil-rich Cherokee."

"The unanimity is remarkable."

"One store remembered her suit as 'sort of lemon-lime'; the other two caught Lois's Bahama Sand shade. Not a single one of the salesgirls noticed her gold-coin necklace."

"A tribute to the power of perception. What about the phone number?"

Sibyl sighed. "Honestly, it's discouraging to quiz people about something that happened last Saturday, Don. They try so hard to recall and they fail so wretchedly. But our gypsy maiden did use that same stunt everywhere she went. And all the clerks and section managers who heard her mention the number agree that there were two sevens and an ought in it —oh, seven, seven something . . . or something, seven, oh, seven. I realize it would take an electronic brain to test out all the phone numbers in New York which include two sevens and an ought . . . and hit the jackpot." She did smile, then, wearily. "Just to play safe I asked Information for the number of Grand Luxe Restaurants—there isn't any. Peter the Great's corporations—there are a dozen of them, at least—are all Baskoulos—Baskoulos Frozen Foods, ditto Epicured Meats, ditto Grand Luxe—Baskoulos this and Baskoulos that."

"Gentleman has a well-developed ego. No wonder it irks him to have his wife gossiped about; it maligns his masculinity."

"Especially," she nodded, "when the other man is small and bandy-legged and homely—if the sports-page cartoons of Hay-Hay Greld aren't too exaggerated. Do you have any other immediate chores for me?"

"Not unless you class having lunch with me as such."

"I can't, Don. I have to go to Edith—you understand."

"All right. Tell her I am confident we'll have news of Timmy before long."

"Are you?" Sibyl frowned. "Why are you?"

He couldn't show her the note now; it would only increase her worry. "Mainly because of the boy himself. Timmy has a lot of stuff on the ball, sugar. He'll be in there pitching no matter what he's up against; it wouldn't surprise me if he did cash in on part of that reward."

"Damn the reward. I wish he had never heard of it. Do you want a Loss list for circularization?"

"No. I don't expect that merchandise to be resold."

"You don't!"

"I think it was taken for personal adornment."

"Two dozen nylon shorts? Enough genuine cashmere socks to outfit a company of Marines?"

"That's one of the things that made it seem likely Ambletts was rooked by a pair of gypsies. The women often wear sleazy, shapeless clothing because it's part of their poor act: if they look as prosperous as they are, they'd never get big tips from their tea-reading clients or their palm-reading suckers. But the men . . . 'they toil not, neither do they spin, yet Solomon in all his glory was not arrayed like one of these.' "

Sibyl stared. "Her total take from all four stores was close to nine thousand dollars' worth of merchandise. You mean all of that for one strutting peacock?"

"I have seen women walk out of our French Shop with at least that much on their backs," he said. "Tell Edith we are doing everything possible."

Everything, he thought after she had gone, meaning nothing, until five o'clock. Though he was under no illusion as to the swindler's probable intentions. The gypsy would know that a promise of *nolle prosequi* made by the Chief of Store Protection was hardly equivalent to a pardon from the Governor. Whatever course Ambletts might take, there were still the other stores she had tricked to be reckoned with. Not to mention the police—anyone clever enough to devise such a scheme and brazen enough to carry it through would be aware that the police could not be bought off with a promise. So the implied agreement to let Timmy go home was not in good faith. The swindlers were playing for time.

Time for what? To put over another coup or two? To get out of the country to some place where extradition would be difficult? And, once the required time had been gained, would the confidence workers dare to let the boy go, possibly to testify against them, later? Also, if they didn't dare to run that risk, what would be the end for Timmy?

He thought about it until lunch time without arriving at any clear-cut conclusion.

He was pondering the unpleasant possibilities as he passed a newsstand on his way to Delby's Chop House—fat black headlines glared up at him from the pinkest of the tabloids:

44

FIND BURIED BOY
(*Picture on Pg. 3*)

He bought a paper, turned grimly to page three. It was a story about a four-year-old buried under a West Virginia mud-slide.

At his favorite corner table he scanned the sport pages, discovered that "Hay-Hay Greld, top-jock at the Florida tracks for the winter season, is expected to carry the Old Plantation colors of that popular racing enthusiast, Peter Baskoulos, to several important stakes victories in the pre-Derby trials at the Keeneland meet, opening this afternoon." The cut of jockey Greld showed a hard-bitten face with a stub of a nose and deep-socketed eyes.

Don was still turning over in his mind the various contingencies which might face Timmy as he returned to the Store Superlative; the more he mulled the matter over, the less he liked it. Why, he found himself asking over and over, would a shrewd impostor who faced nothing more serious than an indictment for grand larceny, put herself in a spot where she might have to face the penalty for kidnaping . . . or something worse? Was something bigger—much bigger—than a score of a few thousand dollars involved?

Which resolved itself into another question: was Baskoulos himself involved—or his fabled millions?

Becky Kahn called out briskly, as he passed her typewriter desk: "Sergeant Lucas on the phone, Mister Cadee."

"Put him on." Lucas was Ambletts' carefully cultivated contact at the precinct station. "What's on your mind, Sergeant?"

"Murder," said Sergeant Lucas.

VI

DON'S AUTOMATIC reaction was: *The kid! You didn't have plenty of time, after all. You fell for that stall about Stryker!* But all he said was: "Where, Sergeant?"

"I'm at the Mid-Broad Building, Forty-sixth and Broadway. I called to let you know you'll be hearing from Captain Dooley, working out of Homicide. Though it might not have any real connection with your store, at that."

"I see, Sergeant." What Don saw was Sibyl with her hands at her throat as if she was having difficulty breathing. She knew Lucas wouldn't have called, except in an emergency.

"You have a Lois Anderson working for you?"

"That's right." He felt a rush of relief that it was not Timmy —then a wave of revulsion at feeling that way when apparently the girl had been killed.

"Thin party? Kind of undernourished? Say hundred fifteen pounds? Ponytail?"

"Sounds like Lois." He saw Sibyl start to her feet, sink back on the sofa.

"She had one of your Mutual Savings Association cards in her billfold. Employee Number four-two-one-three."

"What happened, Sergeant?"

"Somebody put a knife in her back."

"My God!"

"You want to jump over here?"

46

"On my way, Sergeant."

"Come up to the ninth floor."

Don hung up. "The Anderson girl's been killed."

"How?" Sibyl asked in a small voice.

"Knife stab." He knew she would be thinking that a knife was the kind of weapon a gypsy might be expected to use. "Going to meet Lucas over at the Mid-Broad Building."

"What was Lois doing over there when she should have been back from lunch by one-thirty at the latest?"

"No idea. Maybe Frank Wilmar can tell me."

"Do they know who did it?"

"No. Or Lucas would have said so."

"No one saw it happen?"

"I'd say not."

"It might be sheer coincidence. It might not have any bearing on . . . Timmy."

You'd have a different opinion, he thought, if you had read his note. But he couldn't put an additional burden on her, now. "Do something for me, Sib. Scoot up to Advertising, find out if Max Blumenthal has a pipe line to any sports page editors; he buys enough space to be able to wangle an introduction for you, even if he doesn't buddy with the boys."

"The Old Plantation angle?"

"Hay-Hay Greld, specifically. Background, reputation, marital status, associates—particularly his financial record."

She studied him for a moment. "Is this just to keep my mind off my wand'ring boy tonight?"

"It's because nobody stabs a girl to death in broad daylight to prevent identification on the grounds of fraudulent impersonation." He put his arm around her. "It's because Baskoulos looked as if he wanted to kill someone when I saw him in Stolz's office and his wife looked as if she was afraid of being killed." He let her go. "I'm not forgetting about Timmy, depend on it."

47

"I know you're not." The old smile came to her lips for an instant.

In the outer office he said: "Folder on Lois Anderson, Becky."

His secretary, a mousy person with a placid disposition and saving sense of humor, swung around toward the Confidential files. "I hope she hasn't been caught pilfering pillow slips for her hope chest. Girls on the First gave her a shower, middle of March. Some boy in the service."

"That's really rough." Grim lines scored his tanned face. "She's dead, Becky."

"Oh!—isn't that terrible!"

"Don't talk about it." He told her where he was going, added: "Get hold of our friend at phone company headquarters, find out the name of the subscriber at Mulberry nine—seven-one-six-six. Name and address."

Becky made a note. "I'm so awfully sorry about the Anderson girl."

"So am I." Particularly if she was murdered while trying to track down the dame in the sand-colored suit. Damn and blast the bonding company for making a reward offer like that! Probably a girl about to be married needed a thousand more than Timmy Forde did.

Frank Wilmar was behind the Argyle counter where they had talked to Lois Anderson yesterday.

"Miss Anderson take the afternoon off, Frank?"

"She said she wanted an extra half hour for lunch and I let her go late, but she should have been back long ago. Matter of fact, I meant to let you know about it, but I thought it would be better to wait until she'd gone through with it."

"With what?"

"She's off on a fool's errand; I told her so but she got stubborn about it so I didn't want to stand in her way. You see, she thought she had finally remembered the telephone number that gypsy had me call up. Lois thought it might entitle her to some of the reward if she helped to locate the gypsy's confederate. So she dialed this number at least half a dozen times between twelve and one but it never answered. I can't recall the number and I'm supposed to have a pretty good memory; besides, I was the one who made the call for Missus—that is, for that creature who imposed on all of us. But one thing I am sure of and that is, the number Lois tried is not the one I called."

"What was the number she dialed?"

"Why . . ." the Section Manager gazed at the ceiling, examined the pattern in the carpeting at his feet ". . . I had it right on the tip of my tongue, minute ago. Regent four— nine something . . . no . . . well, it'll come back to me in a minute."

"You didn't write it down?"

"No. Because Lois had it on a slip of paper." Wilmar sensed something wrong; he bent low over a pile of gaudily patterned hose, squinting. "I'm sure I can think of it, if it's that important."

"It might be," Don said. "The girl was killed over on Broadway, little while ago."

"Oh, no. No! You can't mean it!" Wilmar seemed stunned.

"Stabbed to death."

"Oh! If I hadn't allowed her to take that extra half hour!"

"Might not have had anything to do with it, Frank." Don touched the Section Manager's shoulder. "Don't brood about it. I'll let you know what I find out."

In the taxi on the way across town, he examined the personnel folder. The photograph pasted on the manila cardboard had been taken when Lois Anderson had evidently been happier than she had been in Menswear, the day before.

At any rate, her job with the Store Superlative had been her first, fresh out of Mount Vernon High School. She had started

49

in Menswear, stayed put, never had requested a change or been refused her raise at six-month intervals. Her attendance record was good, her punctuality beyond official reproach. Sales ability was recorded as Fair, her personality as Excellent, Co-operative.

Details of her domestic life were meager. She lived on West 183rd Street, Manhattan. The Washington Heights neighborhood. Father, deceased. Mother, employed by a Heights bakery. The daughter helped to support an invalid grandfather.

He thought about the hope chest that would be in the girl's bedroom in that uptown apartment. The tissue-paper wrappings on the shower presents. The matching pastel bath towels, the monogrammed pillow slips, the sheets that would never be made up on the longed-for bed . . .

He swore—and the cab driver misunderstood:

"You want me to buy the guy's fender? I'm getting you there as fast as the law allows."

Don said: "I was thinking about someone who doesn't pay much attention to laws, my friend."

There was no cluster of newsmen or photographers in the lobby of the Mid-Broad Building, but when Don said "Nine" to the elevator man, the man eyed him curiously:

"They was a girl stab to death up there on the ninth."

"That's why I'm going up there. Did you take her up?"

"No, sir. But I hear 'em discussing her so I know what she look like and I remember seeing that pink hat by the Directory Board over there. Sure gives you a quiverish feeling to think you might have had a murderer as a passenger in your car, one of those Down trips. Wooh!"

The Sergeant, a tall, weather-bitten man with a sardonic expression permanently fixed on his face, was lounging against the corridor wall by the stair well. The door to the staircase was open.

"Captain Dooley is up there taking some measurements, Mister Cadee. She must have been running away from this guy—he caught her right about the head of the stairs on the tenth floor. After he stuck the blade in her back she fell forward and landed on her face just above the halfway landing. Not the most pleasant picture in the city, but I suppose you want to see her before they take the body away. Go on up. The Captain is the one in the charcoal suit."

He saw the blood before he could see the blanket-covered head. A small scarlet pool had drained from the landing and run down over the next step, like tricklings along the side of a can of red paint.

A flash bulb exploded above him; Don side-stepped the pool of gore; the Sergeant called: "Cadee of Ambletts, Captain."

A stubby man in a dark gray suit squatted on his heels halfway up the flight; he held a peremptory palm up to the two men standing a couple of steps above him, one with a steel tape measure and a notebook, the other with a Graflex.

"See if you can make identification, mister."

Don raised the lower end of the brown army blanket.

Lois Anderson's forehead looked as if it had been bashed in with a sledge hammer. The pink hat that the elevator operator had noticed had slipped down over the nape of her neck—both the hat and the ponytail were spattered with darkening blood.

"This is Lois Anderson," Don said grimly.

"That's what the cards in her billfold said." Captain Dooley stepped nimbly down toward the corpse. "But it saves time to have on-the-spot corroboration." He threw aside the blanket, exposing a soggy stain on the back of the girl's jacket. "Maybe you can supply an answer to this." He knelt, lifting with his fingertips a bit of puckered white fabric nested beneath the dead girl's right elbow. "I've run across a few cases where a

51

strangled man would have a pair of woman's panties wrapped around his throat or used to gag him. But this is the first time I've seen a murdered girl with a pair of men's shorts in her hand."

VII

DON'S EXPRESSION was noncommital, but his thoughts were bitter.

If Frank Wilmar had only let me know what you were up to, you wouldn't be lying there now, like some carcass on the floor of an abattoir. If I had only cautioned you about the danger of making a solo investigation, you'd be at All-Wool Argyles right now. We were to blame, not you.

"She worked in your haberdashery department?" the Captain asked.

"Had as fine a record as any salesgirl on the floor." Don foresaw the line of reasoning.

"Selling shorts like that pair?"

"Sox, mostly." *I'm not about to involve Ambletts in a newspaper sensation, Captain.*

The Homicide man pressed the point. "Maybe she'd been sneaking some goods out of the store. There's a tag on those shorts; they're new."

"You won't find anyone at Ambletts who will believe that, Captain." Don saw a group of newspapermen at the top of the stairs, on the tenth floor. "She couldn't have sold that pair for two bits, through a fence. The only man in her family is a crippled grandfather who probably wears longies until summertime. She had a good job. She didn't need to steal. You can take it from me, her employers trusted her completely." The newspapermen were jotting it down. "Did anyone see her assassin?"

"No one saw her or heard her scream," the Captain answered. "The body was discovered by a postman who was making floor-to-floor deliveries and didn't want to wait for the elevator."

The detective with the steel tape added: "We've canvassed all the tenants on the tenth; none of them will admit having seen the victim alive."

"How long," Don asked, "had she been dead?"

Captain Dooley replaced the upper end of the blanket, covering the wound. "Medical Examiner puts time of decease at around quarter to three, give or take fifteen minutes."

Don drew the bottom of the blanket over Lois Anderson's head. "Was anything taken from her handbag?"

"How the hell can we tell?" the Captain retorted. "There were a few dollars in her billfold, a little change in her purse. Doesn't look like robbery; certainly wasn't a bag snatching. Might have been one of these hopped-up juveniles; good many of them carry spring blades."

They haven't found that slip of paper with the phone number on it, then, Don said to himself. Else they would have investigated to find out whether the subscriber was a tenth-floor tenant. If he told these cops about the fake phone call, he'd have the swindle spread all over the front pages. That might scare the party who's holding Timmy into poking a knife into the kid's back. "Has anyone notified the family, Captain?"

"One of my men is on the way up to One-Hundred-Eighty-Third now. We got her address from an electric light bill in her bag."

Don stepped past the corpse, moved up the stairs.

The Captain said: "Could be a jealousy angle. Quite a few knifing cases involve rejected suitors."

Don said: "A Broadway office building doesn't seem the most likely spot for a girl to be chased and killed by a man she'd turned down." Still, he reflected, the Captain might have a point about jealousy, if Baskoulos was mixed up in this grisly mess. "Let me know if Ambletts can help." He edged past the two plainclothesmen at the top of the stairs.

A pair of *City News* men came over.

"You're from the store where she worked?"

"Is it a fact she was engaged to be married next month?"

"Who's the fellow she was supposed to marry?"

Don said calmly: "You know more about her than I do, boys. Guess you'll have to go to her mother for that dope. I just came over to make identification. Sorry."

He strolled along the corridor, glancing at the names on office doors, trying to see behind the names to a brutal killer. It seemed plain that during her lunch hour, Lois had tried that finally remembered number one last time . . . and that someone had answered, probably giving the correct name of the firm. It wouldn't have meant anything to the salesgirl, so presumably she'd have hung up without disclosing her identity. Then she must have decided to take a look at the person who had answered the phone. From there, it was pure conjecture, except that in the office Lois must have seen the pair of shorts, had evidently snatched them as evidence that she had been right about the recollection, had been murdered to prevent her from telling who and what she had seen.

Theatrical Periodicals, program publishers; *Zuccilato Sheet Music Co.*, your song printed and published; *EssJay Import-ing, Ltd.*, home office Dublin, Ireland; *Sure-fire Records*, Purple Label Hits; *MacReedy Mfg. Corp.*, novelty plastics; *Sol Levin*, attorney-at-law; *Big Ten Carnivals*, charity fund specialists. Maybe there wasn't any business like show business —there certainly were a lot of fringe firms . . .

He came to the end of the corridor, turned back. The door of the *Big Ten Carnivals* opened. A busty, middle-aged woman with bluish hair and a display of bead necklaces that would have pleased a Zulu princess, came halfway out the door, saw Don, retreated a pace.

She peered out at him timidly. "Were you looking for someone?"

He smiled. "Looking for a phone to call my office. I'm from the store where that girl worked."

"Oh." She seemed flattered by the smile. "I guess I'm getting skittish in my old age, letting a nice-looking gentleman scare me. But I've been wearing my nerves outside ever since I saw that awful thing." She moved aside. "You can use our telephone, long's you don't mean to call Honolulu."

"Only as far as Fifth Avenue. Thanks." The office was crowded with furniture, garish with colored posters of caged tigers, bareback riders on white steeds, girls in tights dangling at dizzying heights by their teeth, a diver plummeting from what seemed to be a tower as tall as the Empire State toward a tank the size of a garbage can.

She sat at a desk cluttered with photographs of acrobats and advertisements of Wheels of Fortune. He dialed Ambletts, got Becky.

"It was Lois, all right."

"Have they caught the——"

"Not yet, Becky. Tell you about it tomorrow."

"You're not coming back tonight?"

"Sure, later. Ask Miss Forde to wait for me, unless she has some other date."

"*That'll* be the day! I'll tell her, Mister Cadee. I got that information about the Mulberry number."

"Let's have it."

"It's a bar. Leo's Landfall. Way downtown at Old Slip near South Street. A pay phone."

"Much obliged, Becky. If Frank Wilmar calls, tell him I'll see him first thing in the morning."

He thanked the busty woman, was beamed upon with an invitation to drop around any old time at all.

There was no one in the corridor by the elevators except one newsman, talking to Captain Dooley.

Don punched the Down button.

Twenty minutes to five. No longer plenty of time. The girl was gone; he had to think of Timmy, now.

The city morgue ambulance was at the curb when he hailed a taxi.

He felt depressed, speeding downtown on the West Side expressway, depressed by the conviction that no matter what promises Timmy's captor might have made to the kid, the chances of his getting back to his mother were the slimmest of the slim. For it seemed apparent that the person who had stabbed Lois to death—and Don was by no means certain the Sergeant had been right about the murderer being "a guy"— was tied up with the gypsy in the sand-colored suit.

Yet he could not believe that murder and kidnaping had been used merely to cover up the relatively unimportant crime of grand larceny; he kept thinking of the killer-look in the eyes of Peter Baskoulos.

At the corner of Old Slip he paid off his cab driver, looked for a store which might have a phone booth. A strong smell of fish pervaded the whole waterfront; white-aproned men wheeled hand trucks full of halibut and mackerel, rolled barrels of lobsters, carried baskets of clams.

Red neon lights advertised Leo's Landfall, half a block from the raucous fish market. It was just five.

He went into a ship chandlery, fragrant with new rope, old tar, fresh varnish. On the wall, at the rear, was a pay phone.

57

He dropped in his dime, asked to speak to Mister Stryker.

The barman's hoarse interrogation came over the wire clearly:

"Anybody name of Stryker, here? Wanted on the phone." After a minute: "Ain't here just now, y' might give a buzz later."

Don strode out of the shippy odors to the smell of fish, walked up the cobbled street to the Landfall.

It was a big noisy place with a long dark bar, a dozen crowded tables, a row of shadowy booths.

Nobody seemed to notice him as he ordered Jamaica-on-the-rocks; he didn't appear to be noticing anyone.

Rough-looking customers came and went, singly or by twos and threes, roaring obscenities, bellowing bawdy jokes.

Don was on his second rum when he noticed the man in the canary-yellow cashmere socks. He didn't appear to be the sort of individual who was used to wearing cashmeres; his shoes were cheap, his suit was almost a hand-me-down.

Don went to the Men's to get a closer look at the man as he passed the end of the bar.

He saw the stolid, Indian-like face reflected in the back-bar mirror . . . but then there were a good many men who had Mohawk features and thick, black hair.

But not many of them wore imported Basque shirts with orange and blue stripes as this man did. Not many, either, who had fingernails as filthy——

VIII

DON RETURNED to his drink, brooding at the framed photographs above the bar mirror; ice-sheathed trawlers berthed at the South Street wharves, Bluenose schooners under full sail, a slant-masted buckeye dredging across an oyster bank.

He would be pretty conspicuous in his custom-tailored Cheviot; he would be pretty dumb, too, if he didn't realize that bucko in the Basque shirt was suspicious of him. Still, as far as Don knew, the fellow had never set eyes on him before; he might suppose Don was a plainclothesman on the Pickpocket and Confidence Squad.

The fellow wasn't mingling with the fishermen and marketmen, nor did he have anything to say to the bartender, merely rapping on the walnut with his beer glass when he wanted a refill. So presumably he was almost as much of a stranger in the Landfall as Don; it would do no good to make inquiries of the barmen.

But there seemed a reasonable possibility that the man was the individual who had played the supporting role of the chauffeur at Menswear on Saturday. He had the build to fit in a flunky's uniform, not too tall, not too heavy. Replace that slouchy hat with a snappy, black-visored cap . . . then, the stolid features might not seem so gypsy-like.

The "chauffeur" looked at his wrist watch, called for another brew.

Was he, Don wondered, expecting to meet someone who was late for the rendezvous? Or was he simply waiting for the prearranged time to do something? And why, if all that the swindlers were trying to do was gain time for a getaway, had the fellow bothered to come to the Landfall at all? Had the murder in the Mid-Broad Building altered the gypsy's plan?

Don paid for the rum, marched briskly out to the street, swung southward toward the fish market without a backward glance. One thing was sure: it would have done no good to collar the man on the slender evidence of the shirt and socks, for even if a connection with the swindle could be proven eventually, that would be too late to save Timmy Forde. Not even a session in the back room of some precinct station would be likely to bring out the whereabouts of Sibyl's nephew.

Only thing to do, he thought, was to trail this "chauffeur," if it was possible. He might, just might, lead the way to the place where Timmy was held prisoner.

Don turned the corner at the end of the cobbled Slip, made a fast circuit of the block until he reached the corner north of the Landfall. A pair of bargemen swaggered happily, arm in arm, out of the saloon, singing: "Yes sir, she's my baby." But no Basque-shirted "chauffeur."

Don strolled half a block further north, stepped into the alcove that served as a hallway to the stairs going up to the second floor of a rooming house. *Special rates for maritime singles.*

He waited until nearly quarter to six before he saw the orange and blue striped shirt emerge from the saloon. For a moment the man stood, glancing this way and that, indecisively. Then he walked rapidly up the Slip, toward Don.

Figures he's going to be tailed, Don decided.

The man came on, crossed the street, headed north past the rooming house.

Don retreated up the stairs. A fat woman in a grease-stained dress came to the head of the stairs. "We're full up, mister." She turned her head, looking at him out of the corners of her eyes. "Say, you wasn't *looking* for a room, was you!"

"I'll try somewhere else." He took his time about sauntering out to the street.

The "chauffeur" was just turning the next corner, westward. He didn't look back.

Home-going office employees, customshouse clerks, and factory workers crowded the sidewalks, making it more difficult to keep the "chauffeur" in sight. Making it more difficult, too, for him to spot a shadower.

North at the next corner. West again. And North once more. Into the financial district.

Don lost him at the turn into William Street, made a gambling guess, picked up his quarry again at Hanover, followed him at closer range across Broadway, into the wholesale and warehouse district. Halfway along a block where raised shipping platforms took the place of sidewalks, where moving vans rumbled slowly behind sixteen-wheeler tractor trailers in a snail's parade, the man suddenly vanished. One moment he had been legging it past an ancient warehouse, the next instant he was nowhere in sight.

Don increased his pace, but by the time he had reached the spot where he had last seen the man, almost a minute had elapsed.

Enough to let the fellow hide somewhere down that dark alley.

The alley, cutting between two shipping platforms, was scarcely wide enough for a man to walk without scraping his shoulders against the bricks on either side.

Not the best place in the world to go hunting for a man who might be expected to carry a knife. Still, it wasn't really dark yet. And there were truckers and warehousemen all around here.

But he took good care, when he reached the widening of

the alley, where the wall of one warehouse extended a dozen feet beyond the other, to make a quick leap beyond the corner of the building at his left.

It had been an unnecessary precaution. The fenced-in area behind the warehouse was higgledy-piggledy with empty crates and small scraps of rubbish. But there was no place where a skulker could find concealment. The steel doors at the rear of the warehouses were all padlocked. The board fence, topped with barbed wire, was too high for a man to get over without a ladder or——

That pile of crates at the corner where the fence meets the warehouse wall! Stack one on top of another—an agile man might be able to climb over without ripping the seat of his pants!

Don moved past the coils of rusty wire and pyramids of broken boxes, set a washing-machine crate on one that had originally contained a gas stove, climbed gingerly up, looked over.

Backed up to the board fence were six big red refrigerator trucks. A man could easily have stepped down onto the cab of one of those trucks.

Beyond a wide turning area for the trucks was the rear of another warehouse on the next street. The "chauffeur" had known he had been followed, had given Don the slip neatly.

He dropped to the ground, had not recovered his balance when a harsh voice spoke, almost in his ear:

"You nosy son of a bitch, Cadee! Why don't you stay out of this before you get the kid killed!"

The "chauffeur," on the other side of the fence, not more than an arm's length away! He'd been hiding behind one of those reefer trucks!

Don called: "Make a deal with you."

Silence from the other side of the boarding.

"Hear me? I'll make a deal, for the boy's return."

Still no answer. The man had gone . . . or wasn't prepared to dicker.

But Don was sure the fellow wouldn't have bothered to give that warning unless Timmy was still alive. There might still be time to save the boy.

He went back to the narrow alley, through it, hurried to the platform-skirted street. Another of the big red reefers was rolling past the corner. On its side, in bold black lettering:

RESTAURANTS GRAND LUXE
CHOICE OF GOURMETS
FROM
COAST TO COAST

Surely it was beyond coincidence that the "chauffeur" for the fake Mrs. Baskoulos had led him straight to a warehouse of the Baskoulos chain. But Don could not fathom the connection.

He followed the refrigerator truck, which swung in behind the huge concrete structure with *Grand Luxe Commissary* #7 across the top of the building.

Steps led up to the sidewalk platform; he used them. An elderly man in a mackinaw and straw hat sat at a desk overlooking the truck driveway. Don did not indulge in preliminaries:

"Looking for a guy in an orange and blue shirt. Yellow socks."

"Joe." The man pushed the straw hat back off his forehead. "What you want him for?"

"Joe what?"

"Maginn. I guess his name is actually Yosef, not Joe."

"Work for you?"

"Sometimes. Mends copper kettles, solders fry pans, like that."

"Live around here?"

"You a detective?"

"That's right."

"Then you ought to know how these gyppos are. In and out, all the time. We pay Joe by the job, you couldn't hire him by the day; you'd never know when he would show up. And chances are he lives here this week and somewheres else, the next. They won't stay put any length of time. What you want him for?"

"Questioning." Don didn't make it sound brusque. "Is Maginn married?"

"Search me. Now you come right down to it, I don't really know one damn thing about Joe, except he's a good copper-smith."

"Does he show up here every day?"

"Nope. Comes around every so often to see if we've got any pots need mending. Might not see him again for a couple of weeks. Want me to tell him you're looking for him?"

"He knows it. But you might call me if he shows up to-morrow." Don took out one of his Ambletts cards.

The commissary man examined the pasteboard. "You're not a *real* detective, then?"

"Sometimes," Don said bitterly, "I begin to think you're right."

He walked up six blocks before he found a phone booth in a drugstore.

When Sibyl answered he said cheerfully: "Where shall we have our crust of bread and sip of wine, to discuss the affairs of Hay-Hay Greld?"

"Can't have dinner with you, darling. I've made a date with Bobby Parnell—he's Max's sports desk contact—to get the inside and low-down on the son of Scorpio."

"Son of a . . . *who?*"

"Scorpio. Gentleman who's burning up all the track records was born on Halloween, some thirty years ago . . . under

64

the sign of Scorpio. According to Parnell, Hay-Hay makes a point of living by the same sign, consults the stars before he accepts a mount, has his horoscope served on toast every morning."

"Find out if he ever consults gypsies, Sib."

"I'll try to. There's something definitely offbeat about Hay-Hay the Great; Parnell didn't want to go into it on the phone but I gathered there's a scandal brewing."

"It's past the fermentation stage; it's ready to explode," Don said. "Where can I get hold of you, later?"

"At Edith's. I'm going right over there, soon's I have finished pumping Bobby Parnell. She's already blown up; soon as she heard about Lois she was sure the same thing must have happened to Timmy. So she called the police."

"Oh, great! She'll spill the whole story—about the swindle —Missus Baskoulos . . ."

"I can't stop her, Don. Timmy's her child, not mine."

"Cops will tie his disappearance to the Anderson stabbing. They'll be rounding up all the gypsies in the metropolitan area."

"She doesn't care what they do as long as they help get Timmy back, safe and sound. Neither do you, Don."

"No, of course not. The boy comes ahead of everything else. But she may be doing the wrong thing. And it sort of puts the pressure on . . ."

"I don't see," Sibyl retorted, "how it can be any greater."

"Not on you or Edith, no. What I had in mind was pressure on someone else. I'll ring you at your sister-in-law's, hour or so."

"Don, I'm scared to death."

"I'm not," he lied. "Timmy will be all right, you wait and see."

"I'm worn out with waiting," she said. "I want to *do* something."

IX

"MADAME REGRETS she is not able to see you." The white-aproned maid blocked the door of the Baskoulos apartment.

"She will be able to see me; I am not invisible." Don made no move to force his way past the maid. "Tell her the police will be here shortly; she had better talk to me, first."

The maid was alarmed. "Madame is grieved." She shut the door hastily.

Grieved, he repeated silently. But not as heavy with grief as the small suburban house where Timmy's mother will be on the verge of a breakdown. Not as filled with grief as the apartment on Washington Heights where a crippled old man and a widow will be mourning. For that matter, not nearly as grief-stricken as that hiding place where the boy waits for a release that may never come. He thumbed the buzzer angrily.

The door opened; the maid did not reappear. A tall, sparse man, in his late thirties, Don judged—with a long, leathery face which looked as if it had been narrowed in childhood by being squeezed between a door and the jamb, as certain primitive people place weighted boards on the heads of infants to produce a fashionably flattened skull—smiled apologetically. "Come right in, sir." He held out a long, aristocratic hand. "I'm Sheppard Jefferson; I run the Old Plantation for Peter; I suppose you could call me his major-domo."

"Is Mister Baskoulos here?" Don found the man's hand-clasp firm and friendly.

"No, he's not. But I'm off to Kentucky tonight so I stopped around to have Missus Baskoulos' instructions on *Samatan* and *Merry Lea*; she owns some of our string, you know. But she's too indisposed to discuss their chances for the stake races. So you can understand she won't be able to talk to you. What is this about police?"

"A matter of murder, Mister Jefferson."

The manager of Old Plantation Stables put a palm alongside his face as if he were leaning against a tree trunk for support. "Someone she knows?"

"Someone she knows about. A salesgirl at Ambletts."

"In that case I am sure she will want to be told." Jefferson hosted Don to an easy chair by the huge fireplace, excused himself, called: "Mitzi."

The maid appeared, chastened. Jefferson spoke to her in a low, urgent tone, rejoined Don in front of the crackling oak logs:

"Does Peter know about this, Mister Cadee?"

"Doubt it. Where is he, now?"

"Just about arriving in Washington." Jefferson consulted the grandfather's clock beside the door to the dining room. "Annual banquet of the Boniface Brotherhood tonight. I have to be shoving off myself in a moment but perhaps I should try to call Peter first?"

"I should think that would be up to Missus Baskoulos." The magnificence of the Baskoulos living room made him think regretfully of Sibyl's cozy apartment down in the Village. The elaborate console, with the giant television and the stereophonic apparatus for reproducing records—the contrast with Sibyl's tiny hi-fi was not entirely in favor of the more showy equipment. "She will know where to get in touch with her husband?"

Jefferson fussed with bulldog brier and pouch. "Yes, oh yes. Peter has a house there, Carnavon Circle. Just as he has one in London, one in Athens. Right now he's making arrangements to buy another farm in the Bluegrass." He lit the pipe contemplatively. "He believes in living on a large scale, you see. Sometimes it's a little hard on her; she would like to settle down . . . Peter hopes he will never have to."

From the end of the living room, Rina Baskoulos said with forced lightness: "Now, Shep! Mister Cadee will think Peter's been treating me badly; you know that's not so." She wore a low-cut, bare-shoulder gown of sea green; she seemed more like the ravishing blonde of Bob Stolz's description than when Don had seen her before.

Jefferson gestured with the stem of his pipe as if it were a blackboard pointer. "Peter has so much restless energy, such boundless drive, that it is hard for him to understand why other people don't want to zoom around the way he does. He leaves me limp with exhaustion, time and again; it's a tribute to his personality that people not only put up with that sort of thing but adore him in spite of it, as you and I do, Rina." He went to her, took one small hand in both of his, bowed low. "I'll be at the club, packing, if you need moral support, my dear."

"Thank you, Shep." She managed a smile. "Luck at Keeneland."

He took his hat and coat from Mitzi, touched his fingers to his forehead, saluting Don. "I hope to meet you again, sir, under happier circumstances." And he was gone.

Rina Baskoulos came close to Don. "Why have you come here again? To frighten me with this talk of murder and the police?"

"You remember the salesgirl I told you about? The one who was so excited about having sold so much to the famous

68

Rina Baskoulos, who was so shocked to learn she had been dealing with a swindler?"

"She was the one . . . ?"

"Stabbed to death this afternoon. At the time she was killed she was holding one of the pairs of shorts bought on the strength of your credit coin, your identification cards. She had tracked down the impostor somehow; she was butchered to keep her from exposing the fraud. You were partly responsible for that girl's death."

Rina did not look "indisposed"; she looked like a sick woman; she tried to speak, could not.

"I mentioned one of our stock boys who saw the girl who had impersonated you. He set out to find this gypsy—evidently he did. Now he is being held captive, may have his throat cut at any time—and you will be partly responsible for that, too, if it does happen."

"Why blame me for these horrible things?"

"Because you fed me a bunch of lies when I came here before to inquire about the loss of your credit coin. Because you knew who had taken the coin and your handbag; if you had told me, then, we might have had the swindler in custody long since. But you're going to tell me now, so we can save that stock boy's life, if it isn't already too late."

She began to cry.

Don said: "Even if you don't have a child you can understand how that kid's mother feels. She's crying *her* eyes out right now, thinking she will never see him again."

Rina clutched at the V of her gown as if she meant to rip it apart. "It won't do any good to tell you——"

"Why not?"

"I don't really know who the gypsy is—anyway, she's gone."

"Gone . . . from where?"

"That awful fortuneteller place where I went to see her.

Just a dirty, old, empty store, really. She had told me to go home and lie down after she had taken the curse off the money by burning it, but when I got home I found my wallet was gone, so I took a taxi right back down there . . ."

"Your wallet?" He remembered what Sibyl had found out about the bag the gypsy had used in the impersonation at other department stores. "What about your handbag?"

"She didn't steal that—I said she did because no one would have been able to understand how I could have lost the wallet and the credit coin and other things while I still had the bag."

That gypsy must have been clairvoyant, sure enough, if she could recall that ostrich handbag well enough to be able to locate a duplicate, he mused. *And why in hell would she want to duplicate it?* She could have gotten away with her fraudulent scheme without the aid of that small stage prop, couldn't she? *Why take all that trouble?* Don kept his thoughts to himself, merely inquiring: "Where was this empty store?"

"One-oh-two Harkover Street—she called herself Madame Marbola, Priestess of Peace of Mind—but when I got down there the last time, she had gone—cleared out completely— there was only the empty store. She had moved out in less than an hour; nobody around there seemed to even remember that she'd ever been there at all, with the sign of the zodiac on the door and that brass pot she burned the money in . . ."

It took ten minutes of sobbing to get the story out—her sleepless nights because of "something she had done" to wrong her husband, the fortuitous discovery of the Priestess' advertising card, the first visit during which Madame Marbola had correctly told her many things no one could possibly have known about her, the questioning as to the money her husband had given her during the time when she had been "wronging" him, the judgment that it was the money—the money made evil because of the circumstances—which should be destroyed to restore peace of mind . . .

She had been, she said, too overwhelmed at the belated discovery of how she had been gulled, to know what to do. Of course she couldn't tell her husband—that would have entailed an explanation of the "wrong"—would have involved someone else who was very near and dear to her. So she had made up the incredible yarn about the Degas at the art dealer's . . .

Don believed her, as far as the story went. But it didn't go far enough—nowhere near. The gypsy woman—no doubt her name was something other than Marbola—would have known that Mrs. Baskoulos would be able to describe her, to pick her out of a police line-up if necessary. So there had been no point to committing murder to hide her identity, none to kidnaping the boy. Quite the opposite; the fact that the gypsy would have realized that an attempt at identification would surely follow the commission of a felony—that, in itself, would have deterred the swindler from taking such a possibly fatal gamble as murder or kidnaping.

The sum of money which had been "burned"—likely it was burning a hole in the gypsy's pocket right now—was impressive, but even thirty thousand dollars was not sufficient to offset the risk of the electric chair. Besides, the Priestess had the money, he reminded himself. *She wouldn't have stabbed the Anderson girl to protect it. There was something else, something bigger—*

He had an arm around the shaken woman when they heard the hall door open suddenly.

"Ah," said Peter Baskoulos, scowling. "Hah!"

Don didn't remove his arm. "You might call your doctor, Mister Baskoulos. Your wife has had a severe shock."

"It will be nothing," growled the Greek, "compared to the one which is coming."

"Peter," she cried piteously. "You're mistaken, if you think——"

He cut her short. "Hayworth has been here again; I know all about it." He strode to the stereophonic hi-fi TV console, swung it away from the wall.

"No one has been here," she wailed, "except Shep and Mister Cadee. Ask Mitzi."

"Mitzi is disloyal." He stooped over the rear of the reproducing set. "Mitzi is fired. I have here a more truthful witness." He held up a small spool of silvery wire.

Oh, brother, if he replays that and hears how she's been taking her hair down for the last fifteen minutes!

The blonde must have had the same thought. She ran at her husband, snatching at the roll.

The Greek held her off with one hand. "I've got you cold, my treacherous trickster. I'll get Greld, too, presently—I promise you—and no one will protest when I let them hear what is on this."

She struggled fiercely for the roll of wire. He swung her off her feet, toward the fireplace.

There was a flash, a piercing scream. Flame lashed up from her gown, whipped at her shoulders, her neck.

Baskoulos held her tightly, in spite of her screeches.

Don stepped in, swung from his hip, hit the tycoon flush on the point of his jaw, was tearing the blazing dress from her back before the big man toppled against the fire set.

X

IT WAS lucky, Don thought, that she had been wearing practically nothing underneath that sea-green satin. No slip, nothing but a Bikini-like panty girdle and bra.

The dress lay burning on the black-tiled hearth, sending up a noxious cloud of yellowish smoke. Rina Baskoulos crouched by the big divan, whimpering and clasping the back of her neck; the smell of singed hair was strong.

The maid ran in, mewling consternation at the sight of her half-naked mistress, the sprawled, disheveled figure of Peter Baskoulos. "Oh! Oh! Oh!" She put clenched fists to her temples. "What . . . ?"

"An accident." Don retrieved the spool of wire. "Her dress caught fire. He rushed to help her, stumbled against the mantel."

The maid whipped off her tiny apron, thrust it at the crouching blonde. "Will Mister Baskoulos be all right?"

"In a few minutes." Don stamped out sparks dancing across the smoldering fabric. "But if you know the family doctor's number, call him."

Rina moaned: "No, Mitzi! Don't!"

"Call him; tell him it's an emergency; she's been burned." Don eyed the angry welts on the blonde's back; she looked as if she'd been lashed with a bull whip.

73

The maid hesitated: "Mustn't I bring something for Mister Baskoulos?"

"No. Just help me lift him." Don took the Greek's shoulders; the maid got her hands under his knees. They carried him to the big divan, where he slumped, slack-jawed, his hair fallen into his eyes, his strong white teeth showing like those of some snarling mastiff. "I'll look after him."

"Look after yourself, Mister Cadee." Rina stood up shakily as the maid huried out to the foyer. "Peter will be in a murderous mood when he comes to."

"Judging from those burns on your back, you won't be too safe here, yourself."

"No." She made no attempt to use the apron; she was obviously in too much pain to be embarrassed. "But I shan't be here. I'm going to get dressed and get out. That's why I didn't want Mitzi to call the doctor."

"You have to have something to keep that back from becoming infected." He saw that her face was gray with shock.

"The doctor must come to my hotel, then." She gazed down at her husband with loathing. "I'll be out of here in ten minutes; I should have left weeks ago. That was my most terrible mistake . . . staying on."

"Why did you?" He almost added "since Baskoulos has obviously been so anxious to get rid of you" but let the simple question ride; it was clear enough that something ugly had been brewing in this cozy co-operative—what was not clear to Don was, why had it led to the death of an Ambletts' salesgirl and the kidnaping of a stock boy?

"I thought I owed it to Peter to stay, even after we had quarreled."

"About Hay-Hay Greld?"

She ignored the question but touched a blistered spot on her shoulder, biting her lips to keep from crying out. After a moment of agony she said tightly: "I thought I might atone

74

for it by . . . staying with Peter. I should have known better; you have to pay for your mistakes with unhappiness—you can't just hope to live them down."

"That what the gypsy told you?" He pushed the enormous television-stereophonic, hi-fi, all-wave radio set back against the wall.

"No." She shivered. "That horrible creature! She said I was burdened with a sense of guilt that kept growing heavier all the time—and of course that was true—so I was ready to believe her when she said I could get rid of it if I would do just what she said." She turned, walked unsteadily toward the far end of the long drawing room, her head twisted to one side with suffering. "I have to put on some clothes. You had better go before Peter comes out of it."

Mitzi came in, crying: "Doctor Soames is on his way; he'll be here in five minutes."

Don said: "Get some towels. Ice in a basin. Soak the towels; bring them here." He followed Mrs. Baskoulos to the door of her bedroom; when the maid had rushed back into the kitchen he said: "How did you learn about this gypsy?"

"I told you." Rina's voice was muffled behind a closet door. "I found her card."

"Where?"

"Why—in our elevator, on the floor of the car. It was black with white letters; I'd never seen a business card like that before, so I was curious."

"A printed card?"

"No. Handwritten in white ink. *Madame Marbola, Priestess of Peace of Mind* . . . it seemed almost a miracle that I should find it, for the one thing I wanted more than anything else in the world was . . . that."

A miracle! he thought. A miracle of planting the card where this gullible woman would be sure to see it. "See anyone else in the store on Harkover Street?"

"No. When I first looked in, the place was empty. But just as I was turning to go away, this woman came out and beckoned to me. That seemed providential, too, for I had been so dreadfully disappointed to find no one."

Providential, hmmmm! "What'd she say to you?"

"That she knew I was carrying this heavy burden, that it was possible she might lift the load from my soul because she had been given this strange power to conquer evil. And she showed me the jug."

He spoke to Mitzi in an undertone as she hurried in with a yellow plastic basin. "Wring 'em out, put 'em on his forehead, don't let him get up until the doctor comes."

Rina came to the bedroom door; she wore a dark skirt, held out a suit jacket for him to help her with. "The only thing in this dirty old store—aside from a couple of old canvas chairs—was this gallon jug of muddy water on the floor near the wall. Madame Marbola knelt down before it, spoke to it as if it were human: 'Tell me true, can I clear up this person's troubles?' Then she slapped her hand down on the filthy cork and—in a second, that cloudy water in the jug was clear as gin."

They really put on a show to hook you, sister. "You only went there twice?"

"Just twice." She grimaced as the lining of the jacket touched her blistered shoulders. "The second time was to . . . to have the evil money burned." She touched her neck. "You know it really hurts more than this—to realize what an utter fool I was."

"Were you fool enough to admit anything—or to let her guess anything that might give her a blackmail hold over you? Or your husband?"

She backed away a step. "No . . . no! I made no admissions—except when she asked me about the money Peter had given me. I—of course I can't tell what she guessed . . . she seemed to know so much about me, without my telling her a thing."

Mitzi cried out: "Please—you mustn't get up, Mister Baskoulos—the doctor will be here in a minute——"

The Greek's mumbled cursing sounded as if the man were drunk.

Rina seized Don's arm. "The wire—the recording! Give it to me! He musn't get it!"

"He won't," Don said. "It'll be safer with me."

Mitzi screamed.

"Out of my way," growled Baskoulos. He stalked toward the bedrooms, brandishing the heavy wrought-iron poker from the fireplace set.

Again Don had the impression of the snarling mastiff's teeth. He held up a hand, in the manner of a traffic cop stopping an oncoming car. "Before you put on that raving-maniac act again, Mister Baskoulos, one question. Did you have anything to do with that girl's murder?"

It slowed the Greek but didn't stop him. "Murder? What murder? Give me that recording wire!"

Rina slipped between Don and her husband. "Peter! Listen to me! Mister Cadee came here to make inquiries about one of Ambletts' salesgirls who was killed this afternoon—you never gave me a chance to tell you!"

Baskoulos' snarl became a sinister grin. "I'll give you a chance to tell me everything I want to know when I play back that spool. Hand it over—or the police will have another murder or two to ask about. *Hand it over, Cadee!*"

The dull red blotch on the angle of the jaw stood out like a berry stain as he thrust his head forward. He made a rush, flailing down with the poker at Don. Rina took the blow across the side of her neck; if Don had not caught the heavy tool

77

and parried the impact it would have knocked her down. He clung to the poker as a harsh voice from the foyer called——

"Here, now! Hold it, hold it! Stay loose, everybody!"

Two men in plainclothes gray marched into the drawing room without taking off their hats. One was the stubby Homicide Captain; the other, the detective who had held the tape measure.

Mitzi flew ahead of them: "I let them in—I thought it was the doctor—oh, my God!"

XI

PETER BASKOULOS attempted take-charge tactics. "Who the hell are you—ordering people around in my apartment!" He glared.

"I'm Captain Dooley, Homicide detail," the stubby man said mildly. "And this is detective Jim Rickett, Mister Baskoulos." The Captain glanced at the smoldering dress. "We'd like to have your wife's help in identifying a suspect in the Anderson murder."

"I can't, now." Rina spoke with an effort. "I'm waiting for my doctor. I . . . I burned myself—standing too close to the fire—my dress blazed up——"

Don said: "She ought to go straight to a hospital, Captain. She has first-degree burns on her back." If she figures on protecting that big bruiser, he thought, I won't cross her up.

"We're not in that much of a rush, Cadee." The Captain didn't seem too disappointed. "We have one of your section managers, fella in the Anderson girl's department, Wilmar, down at Headquarters Annex now, going over the photographs. But you know how it is; case like this we like to have independent identifications as a check before we swear out a warrant."

Baskoulos flung the poker at the console; it left a sooty line on the limed wood before it fell noiselessly to the thick carpet. "I'll swear out a warrant for you right now. This store dick made a criminal assault on me, few minutes ago—I want him taken in."

"Peter!" Rina closed her eyes, swayed against Don's shoulder for support. "Do you want me to bring charges, too?"

Baskoulos snarled: "I don't give a good goddam what you do. Cadee slugged me so he could steal a spool of recording wire; I want it back and I want him arrested—here and now!"

Rickett and the Captain exchanged cryptic glances.

Don put his arm around Rina's waist to steady her. "I haven't anything on me that belongs to Mister Baskoulos. You can search me or you can take my word for it."

"You're a liar." Baskoulos came at him. "*I'll* search you."

Mitzi smothered a scream. Rina held out a hand in futile protest, but it wasn't necessary: Rickett blocked off the big man with two casual paces.

And Dooley, with a trace of deference in his manner, said: "We realize you swing a lot of weight in prominent circles, Mister Baskoulos; that's why we're trying to keep things on a friendly basis. But we have a job to do and it doesn't include booking licensed investigators on unsupported charges. It does concern the suspects in a particularly brutal murder case. Let's get back on the track."

"What the hell would I know about the lousy murder!" the Greek sneered.

"Where," asked the Captain, "were you this afternoon, say from two to three?"

Don, watching Baskoulos, thought that the question alarmed the restaurant man. For an instant heavy lids screened the arrogant eyes; then the belligerence reasserted itself—the eyes came wide open with anger, the chin thrust forward, the bull neck reddened. "That's *my* business, you bastards!"

Rickett growled: "Here, now, none of that . . . "

But the Captain did not seem to notice the epithet. "It's

our business, because the elevator operator, in the Mid-Broad Building where this girl was killed, described one of his passengers—not one of the tenants—about the time of the murder—as just about your build and coloration."

"Tall, broad-shouldered, muscular," said Rickett.

"Black hair, bushy eyebrows," said Dooley.

"Gray eyes," added Rickett, "rather bloodshot."

Anger faded swiftly from the Greek's eyes; one corner of his mouth twitched in a sour smile. "Look, you bastards"— he savored the epithet this time—"I'm not about to be stampeded into making any off-the-top-of-my-head answers to your questions. When the time comes for me to make a sworn deposition, that will be different: I can show where I was, every minute of the afternoon. More than that, I don't even know where this Mid-Broad Building is. Still more, so far as I know, I never saw this girl in my life. If that's what you came here for, to back me into a corner because of some cooked-up identification, you can run along and play with your fingerprint files and your ballistic microscopes. Just don't bother me anymore or I'll make you eat your badges on City Hall steps."

Thinks he has a watertight alibi, Don told himself. Or is confident he can fix one up, if he needs it. But something else was bothering him for a moment then: *what was that all about?*

"You don't quite get the picture," the Captain was saying. "You may be involved in this homicide or you may not. But your wife is; Mister Cadee wouldn't be here, otherwise. From what the Anderson girl's mother told us, hour or so ago, her daughter was hot on the trail of a woman who'd put over a king-size steal from Ambletts . . . with the help of your wife's credit coin."

Rickett picked it up. "Now we come around to ask you some routine questions and what do we find? You and your wife have been quarreling and somehow she got badly burned. You and Cadee had a go-round and you claim he's stolen some wire-recordings. We give you a chance to explain things and you give us that old I'll-send-you-to-Siberia-because-I'm-so-strong-with-your-Commissioner gag."

Baskoulos was at ease suddenly. He grinned; the outer corners of his heavy brows lifted, giving him a Mephistophelean expression:

"Have you heard my wife's fishy tale about the way she happened to lose that credit coin? Now, there's one for the book. You say you want to take her down to headquarters to question her? Take her; she'll be glad to get away from me and I'll be twice as pleased to be rid of her. But I want that wire recording before she leaves; if Cadee doesn't have it, then Rina has it. It's mine; it's valuable to me; neither of them leaves here until I get it back."

Rina moaned, flung her head back, gasping for air. Don caught her as she was falling, collided heavily with Baskoulos, who had rushed to her. The blonde head sagged limply as the Greek snatched at the pocket of her jacket.

Then Dooley had wrist leverage on Peter Baskoulos, Rickett's forearm clamped beneath the heavy jaw, squeezing the thick neck, making the handsome face a dark beet-red.

The Captain said: "Better get her to a hospital, Cadee."

Don carried her to the divan, set her down gently. "I had to knock him out to keep him from killing her; she meant to leave before he recovered. I'd say you're right, Captain. I'll take her to the Cornell Clinic."

Mitzi cried: "I'll come with you; I can't stay here now she's going, anyway."

"Good idea." Don watched the bulging veins on the Greek's forehead, the glassy stare in the protruding eyes. "Bring some night clothes for her—a dressing gown." His hand slipped behind the end cushion, found the silvery spool where he had cached it after putting Baskoulos on the divan. "If a Doctor Soames shows up, Captain, tell him where to find her."

Baskoulos made strangling noises.

Rickett said: "Yeah. And where will we find you, Cadee?"

"At Ambletts," Don said. "Any time." He picked up his burden, let Mitzi—her arms full of garments whisked off hangers in haste—open the hall door, punch the elevator button.

If only—he thought grimly—if only I could get Timmy out of trouble with no more difficulty than this.

XII

THE DOWNWARD plunge of the automatic elevator brought the blood back to Rina's gray face, to her brain. "Put me down," she murmured. "Please, I'm all right now."

Don said: "You'll be all right in a few minutes; we'll get you in a taxi in no time."

Mitzi put her arm around Mrs. Baskoulos. "Mister Cadee is taking you to the Cornell Clinic, madame."

"Oh, no!" Rina was horrified. "No, indeed. I'm not going to any hospital."

"But Mister Cadee told the police to tell Doctor Soames that's where he is to come." The maid was puzzled.

"All the more reason why I can't go there. If Peter knows where I'll be——" Rina didn't finish.

Don put a hand under the blonde's elbow. "We can fix it so he can't come to your room."

"You don't know him. He will bribe the nurses; he can buy or bluff his way in anywhere . . . " Rina shook her head vehemently.

"But you have to have those burns looked after," Mitzi cried.

"Not in a hospital!" Rina was almost hysterical. "They'll give me a physical examination, blood tests, all that rigmarole . . . and I can't afford to answer all those questions, don't you understand!"

Mitzi murmured: "Oh?" and "Oh!" and "Yes, yes, of course I do." She glanced at Don out of the corner of her eyes.

Don said: "All right; we'll have to get you into a hotel. Where you want to go? The Sherry-Netherland? The Waldorf?"

The elevator door slid open at the lobby floor. Rina started out but, at the sight of a group of party goers in evening dress, she exclaimed in a low voice: "I couldn't walk into a big hotel like this—I haven't even a shirtwaist on. And Mitzi with all those clothes——"

Mitzi wailed: "I didn't have time to pack, madame. I thought that since you were going to the hospital . . . "

A small, dapper man with a brown Vandyke beard and a black satchel strode in from the street.

"Doctor Soames." Rina held out her hands impulsively.

"My dear child." His eyes scanned her professionally. "What on earth are you doing on your feet—you must get to bed instantly." He glanced at Cadee.

Rina said quickly: "I can't stay with Peter one minute longer, Doctor. Mister Cadee is helping me get to a hotel——" She made a gesturing introduction.

Don said: "Missus Baskoulos refuses to go to a hospital, Doctor—perhaps you can get her to change her mind."

"No!" Rina said sharply. "I'm going to a hotel with Mitzi; you're coming along, Doctor." She clutched Don's arm. "Some small hotel, out of the way, where he'll never think of looking for us . . . you must know some quiet place."

The doorman said: "Taxi?"

Doctor Soames shook his head. "My car. Right here." He led the way, helped Rina and the maid into the rear seat.

"Maybe the Vauclair will do." Don slid in beside the physician. "I've been living there several years; it's quiet enough but not very up to date."

"Fine," Rina agreed. "If we can get a suite—fine."

Don gave Soames directions, adding: "Maybe you can arrange for a nurse, Doctor. She's bound to have a reaction; she had a bad time up there for a few minutes."

The physician grumbled: "She's been having a bad time for weeks. On the verge of nervous collapse. What happened?"

"Better get her version of it," Don answered. "Lot of things I didn't understand, myself. I found myself in the middle of a family bust-up, tried to help the injured party, that's all." Likely enough, he thought, she won't want to tell her doctor about having consulted a fortuneteller in her time of trouble.

For that matter she evidently hadn't wanted to tell those Homicide men much about Madame Marbola, hadn't so much as mentioned the gypsy's name or address. Maybe that had been because of the shock of the burns; maybe there was some other reason. He mulled it over as the doctor's car sped to the Vauclair.

There was no way of guessing how much Dooley did know, though probably the Captain was aware that the swindle had been a gang operation. Madame Marbola, Yosef Maginn, the girl with the lilting voice who had answered the gypsy's call from Menswear . . . and possibly the gamine who had delivered Timmy's note to Big Pat.

If one of the gang had driven that knife into Lois Anderson's back, then there was little hope the boy would fare any better. And a knife was certainly a gypsy weapon.

Still, the one thing Don knew about gypsies was that while they might be badly educated, they were nevertheless generally pretty smart. The way Mrs. Baskoulos had been bilked of her thirty thousand proved that Madame Marbola and Company were no exception; the slickness of the swindle at Ambletts confirmed the shrewdness. Yet, from the gypsy's viewpoint, it hadn't been smart to kill the Anderson girl; it had put the

86

whole bunch in peril. Unless there was some unknown factor in the murder equation, it didn't add up.

At the ancient, massive marquee—the Vauclair clung to incandescent bulbs for the exterior display of its name as more in keeping with its quondam glories than showier neons— Don helped Rina out, was concerned at the sudden, haggard lines in her face, a glassy suffering in her eyes. "You don't want to register as Rina Baskoulos?"

"Oh, never." She shuddered. "Never again in all my life. But not as Ardoni; I don't think I am being vain when I say someone here might recognize the name."

Don said: "Mitzi, what's your last name?"

"Lepreaux, with an x, Mister Cadee."

"Then we'll check you both in under Lepreaux." He handed Mrs. Baskoulos over to the doctor. "I'll take care of the registration. You wait at the elevator; only be a minute."

A good thing they know me here, he told himself as he led the way across the once elegant lobby, otherwise they might suspect me of licentious intentions. But Freddy, the night clerk, had taken too many telephone messages from Sibyl to be under any misapprehension.

"Evening, Don." Freddy made a discreet appraisal of Rina, her maid and doctor, arriving at no satisfactory conclusion but restraining his curiosity.

Don leaned over the desk. "Can you fix up my friends with a good suite on one of the upper floors? A corner if you have one left."

Freddy opened his eyes wide. "Why . . . why, you know we'd take care of them if we could, Don. But the house is full to the broom closets . . . did you forget the Archivists convention?"

"Never knew about it. Who are they?"

"Historical bookkeepers, sort of. Very dignified, some-

87

what lacking in *savoir-faire*. Came in this morning, hundred sixty-four of 'em—be here over the week end . . . damn sorry. Isn't a place in the house to put another pillow."

Don looked over toward the peeling gilt of the ornate elevator doors. Rina was being suported by Soames on one side, Mitzi on the other. The blonde was literally out on her feet. It would be sheer cruelty to shuttle her to some other hotel.

"Never mind, Freddy. I'll turn my suite over to Miss Lepreaux and her sister. That's her doctor, Doctor Soames. She's been in an accident . . . may have to have a nurse in attendance."

"Do the charges go on your bill, Don?"

"Keep 'em separate, time being." He started for the elevators. "You needn't worry about being paid. Let them have anything they want."

"And the best in the house, for any friends of yours. How you spell that?"

"With an *x*, Freddy." He waved aside an eager bellboy.

He forbore explanations about the lack of accommodations. The elevator man flicked a glance of surprise at the suffering Rina, at the night clothes Mitzi was carrying, but merely said: "Nice evening, Mist' Cadee."

As he unlocked the door to his living room, Don said to Soames: "My suite, Doctor. Hotel's full up. Some convention. You take care of her, here, as long as necessary. Maid can sleep on the sofa." He had no chance to explain the lived-in appearance of the room; his camera on the living-room table, the fishing rods in the corner by the radio, the magazines and the pile of Confidential reports on the Winthrop desk. For the phone was ringing . . .

That, he decided, would be Freddy, inquiring whether the invalid needed ice water—the Vauclair had been built before the days of piped-in beverages—or extra blankets or whatever a night clerk might imagine a sick person would require.

"I'll pack a suitcase," he said to Mitzi, "and leave you a closet for her things. Take her right in the bedroom." He picked up the phone. "Yes?"

"Don!" Sibyl was excited. "I just talked to Timmy!"

"You *did?*"

"He called about ten minutes ago and Edith is in a sleeping-pill trance so I knew it would be foolish to try and wake her, but she won't need any more phenobarbital when I tell her he sounded just as chirky and chipper——"

"Where was he calling from?"

"He wouldn't tell me—or, rather, he couldn't tell me because he'd trailed those gypsies in the back of their own station wagon and he'd had to keep hidden all the way so he couldn't see the route they'd been taking—"

"But Sib! Didn't you ask him to look at the number on the dial of the phone?"

"Yes, of course. He was in a pay station—Richmond nine—oh-six-two-seven . . ."

"Staten Island."

"Sure. But he couldn't be sure of the name of the street—it's not in a thickly settled section—but Don! He's all right and he's found where these gypsies hang out and he'll be home tomorrow and we're not to worry one single bit about him—isn't that the best news you ever *heard?*"

"It's a load off my mind," he admitted, without letting his reservations creep into his tone. "I'll be over in twenty minutes, Sib."

In the bedroom, Rina moaned piteously.

XIII

IT WAS nine-thirty, though, before Don parked his Buick in the maple-shaded driveway of Edith Forde's white-clap-board cottage in Forest Hills; by then he had come to a disturbing conclusion. Now he was going to have to break the news of Timmy's note.

All the time he had been packing a suitcase—with Rina in his bed, her whimpers subsiding under the apathy induced by a hypodermic; with Mitzi chattering a machine-gun salvo of questions about room service, valet service, and the shops near the Vauclair; and Soames on the phone trying to locate a night nurse—Don had tried to make sense of Sibyl's talk with Timmy.

The call must have been simply another gypsy attempt to stall . . . otherwise the boy would have been on his way home the moment he was free. If Sibyl had known about the note, she couldn't have been taken in—she'd have suspected that her nephew had been speaking with a gun at his back or a knife point at his ribs. Which was going to make it harder for Don to make his belated disclosure.

She might well resent his holding back the information about his trip to Leo's Landfall and his trailing of Yosef Maginn, might feel that if the police had been in possession of the "chauffeur's" name, they might have been able to find the kid before this. And, he had to admit, she might be right.

◄ She had the front door open before he had taken his keys out of the car switch. "Hey," she called, "what sort of a harem are you running, Haroun al-Rashid? I rang you up to ask you to bring a bit of a night cap so we could celebrate—and some French wench answers in your suite!"

"Do I detect a slightly greenish glint in the eyes?" He gave her an un-Mohammedan greeting. "That would have been Mitzi Lepreaux."

"So . . . ?" She tapped the floor with her foot.

"Rina Baskoulos' maid." He explained. "So the Good Samaritan is on the town for the evening. Sorry about the liquor but that's easily taken care of, later. Tell me about Timmy." Coward, he said to himself; cowardly and cruel, to postpone the necessary evil. Still, there was that million-to-one chance the boy *was* really out of danger.

"I was so keyed up when I called you—I forgot to tell you that he said he knew you'd be wondering if he was all right and I was to tell you that he *was* all right and there was nothing to worry about. Of course I told him his mother was absolutely prostrated with worrying, and if he had any feelings at all, he ought to leg it right straight on home that very instant. He wanted to speak to Edith, but when I said the doctor had had such a hard time getting her to sleep he said never mind trying to wake her, he'd see her tomorrow anyhow, and by then he'd have the dope he had started after."

"Say where he'd been, the past twenty-four hours?" He followed her into the tiny kitchen. In the vestibule beyond was a boy's bicycle; from the handlebars drooped a pair of pink boby-sox, the current banner of juvenile masculinity.

Sibyl frowned suspiciously. "I asked him, naturally, but he didn't actually give me an answer. What he said was. 'First I had a tough time catching up with them, and then after, I had an even rougher time getting away from them.' I supposed he meant that he'd had trouble keeping from being discovered in the station wagon; what else could he have meant?"

"I don't know." Maybe the kid had simply been repeating what he'd been told to say by his captors . . . but why would they have wanted him to even mention the fact that he'd been held prisoner? Because they assumed that since the note had been delivered to Don, Sibyl and Edith would have been told about it? Or because they'd wanted to protect themselves against a charge of kidnaping by claiming the boy had escaped from them? In any case, Timmy was smart enough to have indicated by his inflection, if he'd wanted to, that something was wrong. And, if the youngster had honestly been trying to save his mother from the strain of waiting for his return, was it up to Don to destroy that temporary easing of nervous stress? "Anything in the refrigerator to stay a man's hunger?"

"You haven't eaten!" Sibyl exclaimed. "I'll fix something in two shakes."

"What did he say about the gypsies, themselves?"

"He said Steve had been right about them."

"Who's Steve?"

"Steve Liebman, in the class ahead of him at High, last year." She set ham and bread and pickles on the table. "I suppose that was why Timmy thought he'd have a chance to earn that damn reward; because he knew Steve. Steve used to be a gypsy; his folks were named Glornich, or something like that."

"How does one resign from the tribe? I thought once a gypsy, always a Romany."

"Steve's parents were killed in a car smashup at Coney Island seven or eight years ago; his mother was running a palmist's booth on the Boardwalk. The Liebmans—they're a couple that live in the next block—happened to be there at the time of the wreck, and after they found out both the Glornichs were dead, they took the child home with them. Nobody ever claimed the boy, and after a year or so, they adopted him legally. He's a real nice lad; he was on the swimming team; Timmy tried to make it and didn't quite, so he thinks Steve is just about tops. You'd never know, except for his dark complexion, that he'd ever been a gypsy."

"Didn't Edith ask Steve if he had any idea where Timmy might have gone?"

"Oh yes. She did. The first thing. Long before she notified the police. But all she got out of him was that he'd told Timmy that a gypsy woman who dressed as well as that must have belonged to one of the rich families; the necklace of gold coins made him think so, too. And though Steve said he really didn't know much about it because he couldn't even speak the old language any more—he'd forgotten most of what he'd learned as a child—and the few gypsies he knew despised him because he wasn't one of them any longer, still he told Timmy that most of the rich gypsies had relatives living on the Lower East Side somewhere. He said they sometimes owned a tenement themselves but more often leased a store for a few months and then moved out. So the place to begin looking was down there."

Don went to work with the mustard paddle. "Big order, scouring the East Side of Manhattan for a person who'd want to keep out of sight, anyhow."

"Well, Steve did say that those rich families usually drove expensive cars—Cadillacs, Rolls, Imperials—so Timmy might keep his eyes open for a car that seemed out of place in a section where most people couldn't afford to buy gas for a scooter."

"Still, that would be an assignment that might puzzle a pair of cops in a prowl car." He relished the sandwiches visibly, having decided not to tell her of the note . . . at least not until tomorrow. Maybe with the help of this Steve, it might be possible to get a line on Yosef Maginn—but it would not be necessary to tell Sibyl what he had in mind. Maybe, too, by this time Frank Wilmar had been able to put his finger on one of those photographs in the files of Criminal Identification. "I repeat what I've said before: there's another smart Forde in your future."

She made a face. "He's what mother used to call 'aggravating smart.' I'm certainly going to give him a piece of my mind when he comes home . . . if I have any mind left, by then."

"Um. What'd you get from your sports editor besides a good steak?"

"Half a bottle of the best burgundy in Gallagher's cellar . . . and I wish we had another of the same here now." She compromised on coffee. "Bobby Parnell knows Hayworth Greld very well; in fact, he was the first to use the Hay-Hay nickname in his column—'Hey! Hey! Here comes Grel-l-l-ld!' —natural transition to Hay-Hay."

"Gentleman specializes in Garrison finishes?"

"He specializes in winning. Bobby says he's one of the all-time greats. But out of the saddle, he's a prime specimen of *boobus americanus*. It's not that he's just dumb, either; he's both stupid and superstitious; stubborn and credulous."

"Why would a man like that attract the former Rina Ardoni?"

"Bobby says he's so homely he's positively fascinating to women. And he has plenty of personality; the girls hang around him everywhere he goes, off the track. He has the reputation of having the nerve of the devil himself—that sort of fearless individual appeals to a lot of women. Also he's famous and fairly rich and single."

"None of which would make him unpopular."

94

"Well, the fact seems to be that he's not popular with men, Don."

"Result of a swelled head, probably."

"Bobby said it's because Hay-Hay is so muscle-bound between the ears that he doesn't like to talk to men; he feels he's at a disadvantage. That's why he lets his agent do all the talking for him."

"Who's his agent?"

"Ex-prize fighter, Charlie Daw. According to Bobby, Daw is as shrewd as a Yankee horse trader and as tricky as the operator of a shell game. He goes everywhere with Hay-Hay, lives with him, handles all his money, spends most of his time trying to keep Greld from slipping off to some fortuneteller's or astrologist's. Story is, Hay-Hay keeps a special trunk, nothing in it but a collection of those dream books you see in the windows of novelty stores, astrological magazines, good luck omens, junk like that."

"What happens if his horoscope tells him he's going to lose a big race, I wonder."

"You don't have to. It's common knowledge. He refuses to ride. Claims he has a headache or an upset stomach. Happens once or twice at every meet; that's why he and Peter Baskoulos fight all the time."

"Why doesn't he just quit the Old Plantation, then? He's good enough to get other mounts."

"Baskoulos has him signed to an or-else contract. 'Ride in my colors or don't go to the post at all.' And Daw won't let Hay-Hay break the contract. It's gotten so jockey and owner don't speak—their only contact is via Charlie Daw."

"And," Don said thoughtfully, "the Greek's wife. I think you might call that a contact."

Sibyl sniffed. "Do you want a piece of chocolate cream pie? Edith made some to have on hand when Timmy gets back."

XIV

SIBYL LEANED across the kitchen table to accept a light for her cigarette. "Here I've been so excited about Timmy's being all right that I'd let Lois go clean out of my mind. But it seems so horrible that she should have been the one to suffer, when actually she'd done nothing to hurt anyone."

"She found what she went looking for, evidently. Killer thought she was dangerous to his safety, I suppose." It was a strange chain reaction, though; it had been the women and children who had been getting hurt in this thing, so far. Lois, Rina, Edith . . . and her boy.

"Police have any leads, Don?"

"One—though whether it's genuine may be a question." He told her about the elevator operator in the Mid-Broad Building who had described a man similar to Peter Baskoulos.

Sibyl considered. "From what you've told me, Baskoulos doesn't seem like the sort of big shot to have been trailing a salesclerk in a broken-down office building. On the other hand, a man who could watch his wife being burned and enjoy torturing her would be just the sort who might stab an innocent girl to death over some fancied injury."

"He's an odd ball, for sure. One minute all his feelings are on the surface; the next, you wonder if he has any. If he had the slightest reaction to the murder, you'd never have guessed it from his expression. Cold-blooded Caligula type."

"He's not a creature you would deliberately antagonize. As you did."

"Yes. I don't expect he'll consider a punch in the jaw the act of a real pal. He's not used to being on the receiving end when it comes to punishment."

"With his money, he could hire a battalion of thugs to pay you back. Beat you up or——"

"Don't let your imagination run away with you, shugie. If I judge brother Baskoulos correctly, he is much too smart to put himself in a position where someone could blackmail him for conspiracy."

"When a man as powerful as he is gets good and mad, sometimes he stops being smart." Sibyl regarded him anxiously. "Particularly if his pride has been hurt. I'd say you bunged up his pride quite a bit. You watch out; he'll get even with you if he can."

"I'll watch."

"Where you going now?"

"To the store. To listen to the bedtime stories on that spool of wire."

"I mean where are you going to sleep? I'd like to know where I can reach you if I have to. Why don't you stay in my apartment? I can't possibly leave Edith alone till Timmy gets home."

"A halfhearted invitation, I calls it. Now if you were going to be there . . . "

"Hush y' mouf, honeychile. Here's the key. You know where the clean bath towels are—and if you're still hungry when you get down to the Village, there's hamburg in the freezer and lettuce in the salad tray."

He put the key in the change pocket of his coat. "I'll feel like the kid who went in the candy store though he didn't have a penny in his pocket."

"Best I can suggest in that line is chocolate mints in the delft jar by the radio. If you learn anything startling about Hay-Hay from that recording, give me a ring. I'm curious about that romance."

"So's Peter B." He said good night satisfactorily. "You might have breakfast with me."

"You know I won't stir a step away from here before I see that no-good nephew of mine. But if you can wait until Sunday . . . ?"

"That's a noncancellable engagement."

A dog barked sharply in the next yard as his shoes crunched gravel in the driveway. "All right, pooch," he called softly. "No need to wake the neighbors."

But when he put his fingers on the handle of the car door, he was not so sure it was all right. The door was open a fraction of an inch, resting on the tongue of the latch. He was certain he'd shut that door tightly, out of habit.

The car was parked on a level so the door couldn't have swung open. He couldn't recall hearing the click as the door had shut when he had left the car, but he was sure he would have noticed it if the usual sound had not completed the virtually automatic routine of door-shutting.

He tested the trunk compartment; it was locked. He put on the dome light, opened the glove compartment. Nothing had been disturbed. *You're bad as that pooch next door, getting jumpy at a noise in the night!*

He started the motor, backed out, drove past the cross street, stopped halfway down the block. The dog, a black Labrador, followed the car, barking angrily.

The door of a Cape Cod cottage opened to send a shaft of warm yellow light slanting across a bed of flowers, a patch of lawn.

Don leaned out: "Looking for the Liebmans," he called.

"Shut up and go home," the woman said. "I was speaking

to Satan. Go on home, now." She waited until the dog subsided, slunk away muttering canine threats. "It's the second one down, across the street, where the TV's on."

He thanked her, drove on, stopped in front of a square, brick, two-story house. Through a curtained window shone the eerie blue of a television bulb.

He went along a flagstone walk, rang the doorbell.

Satan growled menacingly, away in the darkness.

The front door opened three inches. A bald head, the continuation of a browless forehead so that the man's pale features might have been modeled after a peeled Idaho potato, appeared in the crevice. "Who you want?" It was a timid, high-pitched voice which seemed appropriate to the potato.

"Steve in, Mister Liebman?"

"No, he ain't." The door began to close.

"Wait a minute," Don demanded. "I'm from Ambletts, the store where his friend Timmy Forde works." He could see only one cautious eye in the slit between the door and jamb. "What time you expect Steve home?"

"Late." The voice was now more sullen than timid.

"Will you give him a message?"

"Won't be up. Won't see him."

Why the hostility? Don wondered. "Can't you leave a note for him?"

"What about?"

"Ask him to call Mister Cadee at Ambletts as soon as he gets home. I'll be at the store, late. It's about Timmy Forde; he'll understand."

There was an unintelligible grunt; the door closed.

Crabby old coot, Don thought. Didn't say whether he'd pass on the message or not. Or maybe he isn't crabby; maybe he doesn't want his boy Steve to be involved in this gypsy business.

He pondered the possible implications, following the flagstones back to the sidewalk. Steve had somehow helped Timmy to find Madame Marbola. She or some of her tribe might have wormed out of Timmy the name of Steve Glornich. Perhaps a warning might have been sent to the foster parents so no more information would be forthcoming from Steve.

He slid into the front seat, reaching for the switch to the dash light, heard a sudden swish like that of a willow branch being whipped through the air. Pain slashed at his throat. His head was jerked back before he could catch more than a blurred glimpse of movement in the rear-view mirror.

He tried to shout, but his outcry strangled in his throat; his breath was cut off by the wire noose which was being pulled tighter, tighter.

He got the fingers of his right hand on the wire but could not loosen it enough to relieve that terrible pressure on his windpipe. He wrenched to the right, twisting his neck, arching his back—the noose cut into his Adam's apple like a hacksaw.

His lungs felt as if they were bursting with blood; there was a thunderous hammering inside his head. With his left hand he slapped desperately at the horn-rim on the steering wheel. He could not hear the familiar be-e-e-p of the horn.

But then, he could not see anything either. He felt as if he were drowning in a sea of his own blood, blood that was not even red, but black——

XV

THE FIRST sound to penetrate that fluid darkness was the barking of the distant dog. It came faintly to Don's ears over the loud pounding of his own pulse; in the intervals there was a curious roaring in his ears, like the crashing of heavy surf within his skull.

He lay on his back on the floor of the front seat, his head against the foot brake, his legs dangling through the open door by the seat next to the wheel. His legs were cold but for some time he lay motionless, gulping air that burned his lungs like molten metal, before he realized that he was cold because he had been stripped of his trousers.

He still felt the strangling wire around his throat, put up his hand to tear it away. There was no wire, but when his fingers touched the mark it had cut into his skin, it was like rasping sandpaper against an open wound. He lay still for a minute, listening for some sound nearer than Satan. If the strangler was still around he was keeping mighty quiet.

The radium-treated hands of his wrist watch pointed to quarter past the hour; it hadn't been quite ten when he had said good night to Sibyl. A wave of rage swept over him: the garroting had all but cost him his life! Maybe the fellow, who'd sneaked into the back seat while Don was on the Liebmans' doorstep, meant to kill him, had left him for dead.

You haven't had as close a call as that since that sniper pinned a Purple Heart on you, he reminded himself wrathfully. But then he had known in advance how much of a risk he'd been running—and he'd known his enemy. Now he wasn't sure. Had Sibyl been right about Baskoulos' wanting to revenge himself? Had the strangler ambushed Don on orders from the Greek? Had the man in the back seat been the same one who had plunged the blade into Lois Anderson's back? If so, why wouldn't the knife had served to take care of Don, too?

His rage subsided at the thought of the dead girl. She, too, had been struck down suddenly, viciously, but without a chance. He was alive, at least; he had a second chance.

He sat up, gasping for breath, holding to the steering wheel.

The car wasn't on the street; it had been run into the back yard of a big, gable-roofed three-story house. The house was dark; only the faintest light from a faraway street lamp glinted on the hood. He searched the darkness for any movement in the shadows; saw nothing.

He pulled himself up to the seat. The strangler had not only removed Don's trousers, but had also taken off his shoes.

On the rear seat, his suitcase was open; shirts, underwear, pajamas, his light gray cashmere suit, his bathrobe and neckties were strewn all over.

Bastard was hunting for something!

He opened the glove compartment; it had been ransacked, the first-aid kit opened and left on the floor.

He reached up, felt above the sun visor in front of the driver's seat. The spool of wire was still there.

Wallet gone, money gone, keys—no, his keys were still in the ignition switch! But the fact that his wrist watch hadn't been taken was proof enough the throttling hadn't been the work of a thief, a mugger who picked his victims at random.

Who else but Peter Baskoulos knew about that recording

wire . . . or wanted it? Rina and her maid, Captain Dooley and his partner. No one else.

. He got out of the car and stepped onto his shoes; they had simply been yanked off his feet and dropped beside the open car door.

What if someone in that house wakes up and calls the police——or takes a shot at you, just for luck!

He found the gray trousers, climbed into them. No belt! Well, they would stay up until he could get to the store. Once dressed, with his shoes on and with the loud pounding subsiding somewhat, he felt better.

The strangler had taken from his coat pocket some bulletins of the Stores Mutual Protective, a half dozen police flyers covering known shoplifters who had come into town from Chicago, and a copy of the bill Ambletts had sent to Baskoulos on the Menswear items. Sibyl's apartment key was still in the change pocket.

It was that wire recording he'd been after, all right.

He started the motor, put on the lights, swung out of the yard at a leisurely speed in case a prowl car might be in the vicinity.

At the moment, he didn't feel like making explanations to the cops. He circled the block, trying to orient himself; finally saw Edith's cottage and took off with that as a starting point. The man with the wire noose had simply run Don's car round the corner from the Liebmans, parked it behind the first house that had seemed to be unoccupied.

Don drove back to Manhattan carefully; his breathing still bothered him and his throat felt as if it had been slashed with a razor.

When he slid to a stop at the Employees' Entrance of Ambletts, one of the decorating teams was setting up a display in the windows at the corner of the Avenue. Jaunty Streetwear for Jaunty Jeunes. One of the mannequins was tall and thin and long-necked like Lois Anderson; it wore a cocky little pink hat and it depressed him.

Wally, the night watchman, peered nearsightedly through his thick eyeglasses. "I just told them you wouldn't be in tonight, Mister Cadee . . . and here you make a liar out of me."

"Who, Wally?"

"Them plainclothesers. A Captain Dooley, some other guy. I told them they'd prob'ly find you at the Vauclair. That was all right, wasn't it? You still at the Vauclair?"

"Technically, Wally. Yes, that was right." He went past the shipping room and the First Floor Stock and the cleaning women with their mop buckets and scouring brushes. Dooley must have figured out that I managed to get that spool of wire out of Baskoulos' apartment after all, must have decided to find out what was so important about it. *Well, Captain, that's my ticket, too, only I think an audience of one is all that's required for the first playback.*

He waved to Vittorio, following one of Ambletts' Dobermans downstairs on the first round of the night patrol, but avoided the customary discussion of the Yankees' line-up, which was Vittorio's main interest aside from his deadly dogs.

In his own office he drank four paper cupfuls of ice water, dabbed a cold towel on the inflamed cincture at his throat. Then he went back to Becky's desk, fitted the spool of wire onto her playback machine, lit a cigarette, listened:

Music, string music. Brahms. *Hungarian Dances* . . . Eugene Ormandy and the Philadelphia——

Mitzi's voice interrupting, apparently on the phone . . . barely audible over the singing violins . . . "Madame will be unable to keep the appointment this afternoon . . . she is not feeling well. . . . No, no . . . I will call you in the morning . . ."

More music. The stereophonic hi-fi, probably. Dvorak's *New World*, the Boston Pops.

The music stopped. There was an interval of silence broken by the ringing of a phone.

The maid, answering: "No, sir, she is not here; she has not come home yet. No, sir, I am telling the truth absolutely; Madame is not here."

Then Rina: "Thank you, Mitzi."

And the maid: "But Mister Baskoulos knows I was not telling the truth. He knows you are here."

"I simply couldn't speak to him, Mitzi."

"It will make him even more angry, not talking to him."

"I don't care. I've just about come to the end of my rope. He's been so perfectly abominable." A muddled sound of sobbing.

"Ah, now, don't do that. Now, now . . . he is making you wretched, you will have the collapse, if you go on like this."

"You and Doctor Soames are just alike; you tell me I am making myself sick by staying with him but you both know what would happen if I left him."

Mitzi apparently had no answer, for Rina went right on:

"That's what he *wants* me to do, run away. He's trying to make life so miserable for me that I'll have to go, to keep my sanity. And the minute I clear out——"

The telephone rang.

Mitzi's answer was barely aduible: "Yes, this is Missus Baskoulos's residence . . . oh, one moment!" . . . then nearer, clearer: "Lexington, Kentucky, calling, madame."

A pause. "This is Missus Baskoulos, go ahead. . . . Yes, yes, darling, yes. . . . Oh, worse than ever, much worse, you have no idea how much worse. . . . No, not yet, no, but I'm just about at my wits' end . . ." A good half minute of silence, then . . . "I think we've reached the point of no return, darling——something has to give quickly or . . . Of course not, Hayworth, I shan't do anything as desperate as that. . . . No, indeed, I'd rather put something in his coffee than do anything like that—don't forget that——"

The buzzer at the door.

Mitzi, cautioning: "Careful, madame!"

Rina, saying: "Will you be at the motel tonight? Yes? I'll call you there . . . bye, darling . . ."

A garbled voice mingled with Mitzi's greeting.

And Sheppard Jefferson, saying: "Have you a good stiff drink for a diplomat who bears an ultimatum, Rina?"

XVI

"MITZI," THE wire spoke in Rina's voice, "a bourbon on the rocks for Mister Jefferson."

"Make it high tide, Mitzi." The manager of the Old Plantation sounded as if he were giving orders to a barman.

"I'm sorry," the maid was apologetic, "I do not know if we have——"

"Cover the rocks," Jefferson explained. "Plenty of whisky. I need it."

"Oh . . . oh yes, certainly . . . I will fix . . ." Mitzi's voice trailed away.

A door closed, then for a moment there was nothing but the surface noise of the playback apparatus.

Don massaged his throat, asking himself if he had been half choked to death merely to prevent him from eavesdropping on the crisis in the Baskoulos ménage? Was it possible that this emotional blowup had any connection with Lois Anderson's murder, with Timmy Forde's kidnaping? The only plausible linkup seemed to be the gypsy angle, which suggested that the person who had so nearly finished off the strangling job might have been Yosef. But why? What was there on that spool of wire which called for such homicidal violence to prevent Don from hearing it? It seemed fantastic to suppose that Baskoulos would have attempted a garroting simply to obtain evidence against his wife.

"I feel like a heel." Sheppard Jefferson was audibly agitated. "If you want to send me packing before I give you Peter's message, I won't blame you a bit, Rina."

Rina answered wearily: "I've probably heard it all before, Shep; I'd rather hear it from you than from him."

"I'm too embarrassed to give you more than the gist of it: unless you move out of the apartment and so give him grounds for action on the basis of desertion—which, as you know, would cut you off without a settlement or any alimony—he will file for divorce, charging adultery. He says he doesn't want to do this, but——"

"He'd like nothing better," Rina interrupted, "if he thought he could get away with it. Now if he were to sue for alienation of affections . . ."

"Peter's too proud to go into court with the admission that Hay-Hay took you away from him."

"He's too afraid that I'd be able to show who really did the alienating. Peter killed the last of my affection long before I became fond of Hayworth; he knows that the testimony I could present to prove it would make him look ridiculous."

"Can't say I disagree with you in any way, Rina. But before you make up your mind, you have to consider Hay-Hay."

"I have considered him, Shep. That's why I haven't made the break, because I am considering him. Several times Peter's threatened to kill Hayworth."

"I think he will ruin Hay-Hay before he attempts any other revenge."

There was a pause before Rina said: "Ruin?"

"Not financially. Professionally. Peter means to kill Hay-Hay's reputation by refusing to let me put the best jockey in silks up on anything but the third-stringers in our stables. He'll only allow Hay-Hay to ride horses that don't figure to come in the money."

"Hayworth would ride anything with four legs if Charlie Daw would let him—but Charlie won't let him saddle more than a certain number of third-raters. If Peter refuses to let Hayworth take *Merry Lea* to the post, Peter'll be the loser— no other rider can get the stretch run out of *Merry Lea,* that's a matter of record."

"Peter can afford to lose, because all he'll be losing is money. Hay-Hay will lose his rep, don't you see, Rina? He won't be bringing home winners; most of the time he'll be finishing in the ruck. Pretty soon the other owners will decide that Hay-Hay no longer has it, the public will begin to jeer when he comes on the track for the parade to the post, the turf writers will pan him in their columns—all that is bound to have an effect on Hay-Hay; first thing you know, he won't have that magic touch any more."

"Yes, I see," Rina replied dejectedly. "Peter made me give up my career when I married him; he couldn't stand to have me admired and applauded for my own talent; I was to be complimented only for being Missus Peter Baskoulos; that should have been enough. Well, it wasn't—and he recognized it and it infuriated him, lowered his own lofty opinion of himself. Now, to get even with me, he wants to do the same thing to the one person I genuinely like. He can't do it, Shep—he shall not do it." Her voice trembled. "Not if I have to——" she hesitated before adding, "to take matters into my own hands. I won't have Hayworth's life wrecked because of Peter's hatefulness—*I won't, I won't, I won't!*"

"Easy," cautioned Jefferson, "here's Mitzi."

It had taken that maid quite a while, Don thought, to cover a couple of ice cubes with a high tide of bourbon; maybe Mitzi had been doing some eavesdropping, too?

Presently Jefferson said: "I'm supposed to take back an answer to Peter's unreasonable 'or else'; I can't tell him what you just said."

"Why not?" Rina demanded. "Tell him if he doesn't leave Hayworth alone, I'll . . . see to it that he's stopped."

"You know how Peter reacts to threats, Rina."

"Yes. Yes, I do. That's the point, Shep. He never expects anyone else to react the same way. Well, now I have. And no matter what it may cost me, I'll make good on it, you can depend on it."

"Look, now, child——" Jefferson's attempt at soothing her was cut short by the distant door buzzer.

Don regarded the playback apparatus dubiously; perhaps he'd had the picture all wrong. Maybe it had been some emissary of Rina's who had crouched in the back seat of his car with the wire noose—certainly she was the one who had the most to lose by having that conversation repeated before witnesses. Such a supposition made the gypsy angle fit into the puzzle more naturally, too; Rina did know Madame Marbola, might have met Yosef down there on Harkover Street.

Mitzi, breathless, announcing:

"That Mister Cadee from Ambletts, madame."

"Tell him I'm ill," Rina protested. "Too ill to see anyone."

"But, madame, he says the police are coming here——"

Rina exclaimed, "Oh *no!* I couldn't face them." Her words grew fainter as she ran to her bedroom. "I simply couldn't. Shep . . . you handle it so I won't have to."

The buzzer sounded again. Jefferson swore softly. "I'll see what this fellow has to say, Mitzi . . ."

A half-minute wait, before the manager came back within range of the pickup microphone ". . . won't be able to talk to you. What is this about police?"

Where you came in, Don said to himself, switching off the playback and rewinding the spool. He removed it from the machine, dropped it in the top drawer of Becky's stenographic desk. It might be an idea, he decided, to have her run off a transcription in the morning: he had a disquieting suspicion that he had missed something important as he had listened to the unreeling of the recording wire; it was like a well-remembered name that was almost on the tip of his tongue but which annoyingly continued to elude him.

There were reports on his desk which should be initialed, inventory loss reports from the Section Managers of "sick" departments where additional Protection people were in urgent request, the day's gleanings of confessions and admissions to be signed. But he sat at his desk for a long time without touching the papers; the possibility that he had not quite understood the significance of the wire recording gnawed at him.

By quarter to twelve, when his throat had become so swollen that he couldn't stand his collar buttoned, he had come to but one conclusion—and what inference could properly be drawn from it was beyond him. Baskoulos was in a tearing hurry to discredit his wife, to damage her, to divorce her. On the other hand, Rina had been stalling, putting off the evil day as long as possible. She had suffered abuse and indignities yet she had not left his bed and board, as the lawyers put it, until tonight. It was as if she had been waiting, every day, for something to happen which might make the drastic move unnecessary. The same hour-to-hour postponement tactics Timmy's captor was employing; was that coincidence or something more sinister?

What were those damned gypsies waiting for? For the same thing which had kept Rina in hopes that a final break with her husband might be avoided?

Maybe you'll be able to come up with an answer when your throat stops feeling like a red-hot stovepipe. He scooped up the papers, tossed them in his top drawer, went out to the elevators.

Walley touched the visor of his uniform cap. "That was lousy about the Anderson girl, Mister Cadee." He rattled the pink tabloid spread on his lap.

"What's the paper say about it?" Don could read the big black headlines, upside down:

BRIDE-TO-BE
BUTCHERED ON
B'WAY STAIRS

"Ah!" Wally made a derisive pushing-away gesture. "They try to make out like it was a lousy sex murder. Claim she was clutching a pair of men's drawers when she was stabbed. Here, you can have it; all I wanted was to read the picks at the tracks, tomorrah."

"Thanks, Wally."

"You think it was a sex maniac done it?"

"No. Nothing to suggest that at all. That's just to hop up circulation, Wally. 'Night."

He read the lurid inaccuracies by the dash light in his car, expecting to find nothing new.

And was mistaken. At the end of the garbled column and a half:

> A *high official of the Police Department* stated that the autopsy showed the attractive brunette had been stabbed with a thin, sharp blade similar to a surgeon's scalpel.

For high official, Don read "Captain Dooley." No interpretation of the weapon's description was necessary . . . but who ever heard of a gypsy carrying a scalpel?

For that matter, what would Peter Baskoulos be doing with a surgeon's knife?

XVII

HE DROVE downtown, stopping in Sheridan Square to pick up a couple of less sensational papers. Both contained libel-proof references to the men's garment found in the dead girl's grasp; both had vaguely worded statements about her engagement to a sergeant in a paratroop outfit stationed at Fort Campbell, Kentucky. The more sedate of the morning journals reported a brief interview with the grief-stricken mother; her daughter had never been wild or wayward, always hard-working and home-loving—had been liked by everyone. The circumstances of her death were utterly incomprehensible.

They would hardly be more understandable, to the mother, Don thought glumly, if she knew about the peculiar sequence of violence which had followed the swindle at Menswear. The boy's kidnaping, the girl's murder, Rina's ordeal by fire, the near miss of the strangler were obviously all part and parcel of the same coverup. But for the moment, Lois was past the need of protection; Rina was in sanctuary; he, himself, had escaped assassination. Timmy was still in peril.

Anger smoldered within him as Don brooded about that snub-nosed, impudent teen-ager while using Sibyl's key to unlock her apartment. No dodging it: Don might have increased the risk of a tragic end to the boy's life by playing a lone hand, so far, by keeping his information about Yosef

Maginn from the police. Might have increased it still more by not waiting at the office tonight for a phone from Steve Glornich-Liebman . . . if the onetime gypsy were to be allowed to call Don back.

He made himself a stiff lime bacardi, took it into the bedroom, depressed by Timmy's dire predicament. The kid's captors were stalling . . . but evidently not for ransom money, certainly not for any promise of nonprosecution, now. Only rational inference was, they needed time to get away—to take the kid away with them. Away? Where . . . and why?

The rum was molten lava to his throat. After the first swallow he took a look at himself in the medicine-cabinet mirror, was surprised to see an inch-wide collar of black and blue marks around his neck, like some sailor's misplaced tattooing. His prematurely white hair stood straight up like a cockatoo's crest; there were leaden smudges beneath his eyes.

Don't feel sorry for yourself, he told his reflection grimly; you're better off than Lois or Rina, much better off than Timmy. Still, wouldn't you like to have a short session alone with the lad who drew that damned noose so tight!

A long hot shower helped. A second bacardi went down less painfully than the first. He put on the pajamas which the strangler had mussed up, stretched out in Sibyl's bed, drifted quickly into the deep sleep of exhaustion.

And woke—it seemed—almost immediately. Someone was moving stealthily only a few feet away in the pitch-blackness of the bedroom.

He rolled out of bed, landed on his feet in a crouch, made a lunge for a shadow near the bureau.

"Oh Lord, Don!" Sibyl cried. "You nearly gave me heart failure! I thought you were sound asleep!" She snapped on the bureau lamp.

"I was." He blinked at the nylons and lingerie she held.

"How'd you get in here when I had your key—and why the tiptoe in the tulips?"

"I took Edith's duplicate key, the one I gave her so she could stop here when she's in town for an all-day shopping spree." She stared in horror at his throat. "*What happened to you!*"

He told her, toning it down considerably. "Looks worse than it feels, shugie. Why didn't you phone you were on the way over; I'd have had the collins all mixed."

She shook her head soberly. "Haven't time for a drink, darling. I've barely time to catch my plane."

"Now *wait* a minute——!"

"Make yourself a drink while I finish packing." She opened the bedroom door; the lights were on in the living room. "I meant to leave a note to tell you, as I did for Edith; you seemed to be sleeping just as soundly as she was when I left her."

"Tell me what?" He scowled at her huge hatbox, open on the divan, shoes and mules already tucked in the pockets.

"The police came about half past one . . . and *they* nearly gave me heart failure, too." She dashed back into the bedroom, returned laden with blouses, skirts. "A Captain Dooley and a detective; I was afraid they were bringing bad news about Timmy . . . and of course it was, but not : . . . what I'd been so scared it might be. They'd just come from your hotel where they had talked with Rina Baskoulos—*she* told them Timmy had been kidnaped by this band of gypsies."

That's your doing, Don accused himself sourly; you told Rina that; she was simply repeating it. "You let Dooley know you'd talked to Timmy tonight?"

"Yes. They seemed to think that confirmed what they'd learned from Rina. And asked the same question you had asked earlier—how had Timmy been able to locate this Madame Marbola—so when I began about Steve Glornich, they made me take them straight over to the Liebmans to see him."

She's still worried, he decided, but somehow she seems more calm than when I left her at Edith's. As if she'd arrived at some desperate decision. "Did you see Steve?"

"He was in bed. They made him get up. I felt so sorry for him, partly because that Captain Dooley threw the fear of God into him but mostly because he was so terribly upset about having gotten Timmy into trouble. He was sure that if he hadn't given Timmy the dope about the Caddy clan, he wouldn't have been able to find Madame Marbola and her chauffer." She made another trip to the bedroom for hairbrush, combs, and cologne. "Seems that after Timmy had described Marbola to Steve, he guessed she was one of a certain tribe—I don't know what else to call it, because they live more like Indians than anything else—that never drive anything but big expensive cars . . . mostly Cadillacs and old Rolls-Royces, sometimes Buick estate wagons. Steve said that the minute Timmy told him how good-looking the fake Rina Baskoulos was and how smartly gotten up the chauffeur had been and especially about the chauffeur's filthy fingernails, there wasn't much doubt in Steve's mind that they were both from this Caddy clan. Usually the men work as tinkers, fixing old pots and kettles; the grease and grime gets under their nails."

"Where," Don put an arm around her, "do you think you're going, at half past four in the morning?"

"Lexington, Kentucky." She closed the hatbox, snapped the catches with a flourish. "Because Steve Glornich said that's where these Caddy gyps are likely to hang out after one of their women has made a big score off some sucker—at the race tracks. The women steal the money; the men spend it betting."

"I must be slow-witted, being roused so suddenly. Timmy certainly didn't go to Lexington to find Madame Marbola."

"Chances are he went to Jamaica, Don. That's where the horses are running now, in the metropolitan area. The Caddy gypsies generally park as close to the track as they can, as close as they're allowed to, and often they sleep in their cars, sometimes on the ground beside the car with a canvas awning rigged up in case it rains. Steve said you could always tell one of their automobiles by the rolls of bedding and mattresses roped on the roof——"

"You're not taking any plane." He held her tightly.

"Indeed I am. Jamaica closes in a couple of days and some of the horses have already been shipped down to Lexington for its spring meeting. That's where Hay-Hay Greld is . . . and Hay-Hay's been consulting gypsy fortunetellers right along. You can call it a long shot if you want to, but I think it's a good gamble that Madame Marbola is the oracle Hay-Hay has been patronizing. If I'm right, she'll probably be on her way to Kentucky right now, to keep in touch with her paying patron. Whether she and her chauffeur—*and* Timmy— are Bluegrass bound or not, Hay-Hay's there; he'll know how to locate her. Once I know where to find her, we call up the reserves and rescue my best-beloved nephew."

"No." He was firm. "It's an outside chance . . . but you won't take it, Sib. I'll go."

"You will not." She rumpled his hair affectionately. "First place, Captain Dooley wants to see you at the store, nine o'clock in the morning, with Frank Wilmar; I told him you'd be there. Second place, after that awful throttling tonight, the chauffeur would recognize you before you could get anywhere near Timmy—while none of the Caddy clan has ever seen me. Third place, I have to *do* something myself about Timmy, don't you see, darling? It was my fault he started trailing these

117

horrible people; I should have put my foot down right away as soon as I heard him mention the reward. I should have warned my sister-in-law not to let him go . . . and I didn't. So if I don't do whatever I can—right now—to get him back to her safe and sound, I'll never be able to live with myself if anything happens to him. I have to make the try; I'm going to; I know you think it may be dangerous but that's precisely why I have to do it." She kissed him. "Please don't throw any monkey wrenches."

"I don't like it, Sib." He still held her close.

"That means you think I may be on the right track."

"It means that all the females who've been mixed up in this business so far have been hurt. And I don't want you——"

"Oh!" She pushed him away. "Can't you tell that I *have* been? Nothing could hurt me more than to sit on my hands and watch poor Edith go slowly out of her mind, *nothing*." She caught up the hatbox. "I have to fly now, darling."

"Phone me at the store by noon, then, will you?"

"Yes, yes. I'll call." And she was gone.

XVIII

HE BREWED coffee, turned on Sibyl's radio. It would be no use trying to get back to sleep.

He knew very well he shouldn't have let her take that plane. But he realized, too, that nothing he could have said would have stopped her. She had arrived at the point where her sense of responsibility for Timmy's return was greater than her concern for her sister-in-law; that must have been a hard choice for Sibyl to make.

By now the ponderous wheels of police machinery would be grinding out descriptions of Timmy, turning out data on Madame Marbola, clattering the official teletypes with queries about gypsies traveling with a snub-nosed, redheaded youngster in their big car. Was it barely possible that Sibyl, relying on intuition more than on logic, could get to Madame Marbola before the forces of law and order did?

Priestess of Peace of Mind! He snorted; since Rina had made that Saturday trip to Harkover Street, there had been nothing but trickery and trouble, for her, for Ambletts and its Protection staff. It was like the five-minute newscast coming over the radio now, he thought—a gloomy succession of minor tragedies and major disasters, winding up with a sorry little snapper about a London shoplifter who had been grabbed while stealing a plain gold ring on the morning of her wedding day.

No, he told himself under the soothing sting of the cold shower, there was a difference. The accidents and atrocities on the radio were isolated instances, unconnected except through the common perversity and criminal carelessness of man. Lois Anderson's death, Timmy's kidnaping, Rina's injuries were all, somehow, tied together; all bound up in someone's malignant scheme.

He took a clean shirt from his suitcase, unfastened the pins which his laundry had concealed so as to puncture the skin of the unwary. A bit of colored thread fluttered down onto the suitcase lid. A half-inch length of thick brown woolen stuff which must have caught on one of those pins as the throttler made a search through Don's luggage. Tweed, by the looks of it; he was no judge of such fabrics but Frank Wilmar would be able to tell something about the sleeve from which it had come . . . a man's coat, a woman's jacket.

It hurt him to button the shirt at the collar; his throat was swollen; he thought, automatically, of the strong fingers of Peter Baskoulos and the smoldering fury in the Greek's eyes. Still, that rage had not been directed at him but at Hay-Hay Greld. Besides, to jerk that garrote tight wouldn't have required the powerful muscles of the restaurant magnate—any moderately strong person could have done the choking.

He made toast, was buttering the second slice when the phone in the living room rang sharply.

Maybe Sibyl had missed her plane—or perhaps it was fog-bound at the airport; this time of year there were frequent zero ceilings.

It was Edith, sounding muzzy, as if not quite over the effects of a sleeping drug:

"Don? . . . Let me speak to Sibyl."

"She's not here, Edith."

"Then what are you doing there?"

"She loaned me the apartment; I couldn't get in my suite at the Vauclaire."

"But where is she? She promised me she was going to stay here but when I was awakened, a few minutes ago, all I found was this note, and I can't make any sense out of it. She said she'd talked to Timmy and he was all right and would be home some time today. But, Don, he *isn't* all right——"

"How you know?"

"Because somebody just left this message in his cap and left the cap on the doorstep and rang the bell, but when I got to the door—— I don't know how long the doorbell had been ringing; I had a dream about it being the warning bell at a railroad crossing, and my car was stalled on the tracks with the train rushing at me—so when I finally did get to the door, there wasn't anyone there. Just Timmy's cap and this piece of paper in it."

"What does it say?"

"I'll read it to you—I have to keep pinching myself to be sure it's not just something out of a nightmare."

"Timmy's handwriting?"

"No. Looks like a woman's, very neat and regular."

"On ruled notepaper, torn from a notebook?"

"Yes. It says:

> 'He sends you his cap to tell you all is yet well with him but there is much evil in the air. He has come to no harm but the cloud hanging heavy over our heads may burst at any time and end all unless we move, swiftly, like birds at night. And we must fly on golden wings.' "

Don broke in: "How much they want?"

"I don't *know*," Edith wailed. "I can't understand. She says:

> 'We make no demand; a young life is beyond price. But the reward will be his; we take nothing with us when we leave; the things will all be found with him. What he

will get you should be willing to give, for his safety. Send it, in old small bills, by the red-headed aunt; trust no one else. So she must come, alone, at twelve tonight, to Grand Luxe Commissary #7. If she brings the golden wings, she will be taken to the wearer of this cap and all will be well for you and him.'

"But Don," Edith quavered, "what does it mean?"

"They want you to pay a ransom. Now, don't fret up a sweat."

"But the note doesn't say how much . . ."

"They want the reward money the bonding company is offering; it'll come to around five thousand."

"You know I can't raise anything *like* that."

"Ambletts can, Edith. If it's necessary, we'll get hold of whatever is needed."

"If it's *necessary!*"

"If we don't get Timmy back before then."

"Do you"—she smothered sniffles—"do you think he is all right?"

"He was, last night, when Sib talked to him."

"*Oh, I wish she'd waked me up!* Where is she now?"

"I don't know, Edith. But I'll be hearing from her shortly."

"She hasn't gone out of town or anything like that? Nowhere that would keep her from going to that Grand Luxe Commissary tonight, wherever it is?"

"If Timmy's not home before midnight, Sib'll be there and she'll have the flyaway money." He said it with all the assurance he could muster. "Leave it to me, Edith; getting Timmy back safe and sound is my job; by this time tomorrow he'll be right there at home."

"I feel so lost without him, Don, so helpless. What *can* I do to help?"

"Hardest thing in the world: keep your chin up."

"I'll try. What shall I do with the note?"

"I'll be over to get it—or I'll send one of the girls over."

"Will you have Sibyl call me just the minute you hear from her?"

"I sure will, Edith. I'll call you anyway, before long."

He stared at the blue delft jar for a long time, his hand still on the phone.

If it weren't so damned serious, it would be comical—these Caddy-clan gypsies wanting to cash in on the reward for the return of the merchandise they had stolen! What colossal crust!

And the ransom note had such a tenor of trickery, he reflected. The "cloud hanging heavy over our heads"—was that the danger of conviction on the charge of murdering Lois Anderson? Or on the charge of attempted strangling? No, that didn't add up; if Marbola and Company had been mixed up in the murder, no mere greedy desire for another few thousand dollars would have tempted them to run the risk of being trapped by this ransom setup.

Well, getting the money would be no problem, if it came to that. But getting hold of Sibyl might be.

She would be somewhere over the Alleghenies about now; he could wire the airport to have her paged as she left the plane. Meanwhile, he could find out where to get hold of Hay-Hay Greld.

He rang the Vauclair, asked for his suite.

After a half dozen rings, Mitzi answered sleepily.

"Let me talk to Missus Baskoulos," he said.

"I can't, Mister Cadee; she is asleep."

"Wake her up. Tell her I have to speak to her for a minute; it's important."

"The doctor said she is not to be disturbed under any circumstances. She is under sedatives, strong sedatives. I am very sorry, Mister Cadee."

She gave him no time for a comeback. She hung up.

XIX

SORRY, HE repeated, silently. Last time he'd heard Mitzi say it, she'd been lying in her teeth, to Baskoulos. But why would the maid lie now, to Don? Yet she must have been; she hadn't even said "in an hour or so" or "I'll call Doctor Soames and see."

He dressed swiftly, slid the butter back in the refrigerator, ate the toast on the way down in the elevator. It was five-thirty when he parked in the "No Parking" zone at the Vauclair.

The lobby, ordinarily deserted at that hour, was now ahum with Archivists. Freddy wasn't at the desk. Don went up to his suite, rapped on the door where the "Do Not Disturb" sign hung.

It took a wait and prolonged knuckling before Mitzi inquired, "What is it?"

Don said: "I have my key, Mitzi; I'm coming in anyhow if you don't open the door."

"Oh! Mister Cadee! One moment." She let him in; she wore one of Rina's peignoirs over a pale blue nightgown. "If you wish something from your bedroom, permit me to bring it to you so Madame will not be——"

"You forget," he said, "I've already seen your mistress undressed; it won't hurt for me to see her in bed." He moved toward the bedroom.

"No, no, please! Tell me what you want." She flung out her arms to bar him from entering.

Don caught her wrist, pushed past her. The bed was rumpled but Rina Baskoulos was not in it. "What I want is the truth. Where'd she go?"

"To . . . Kentucky." Mitzi was scared. "By airplane."

"When Soames didn't even want her to stay out of bed five minutes; come on, now."

"It is so, Mister Cadee. The doctor, he goes with her, but he does not like it. He told her she was taking a terrible chance. Then she let him go along, too."

"How long ago was this?"

"They left about two. She slept a short while; then after the policemen came, she could not go back to sleep. She is in much pain and very upset; she made me call the doctor to come right over. When he arrive, they argue, they disagree— oh, for a long time—but Madame, she make him see the point. So the doctor goes with her."

"Why the mad rush?"

"She is afraid Mister Baskoulos, he is going to kill Mister Greld. She make me call the apartment; Mister Baskoulos is not there. I have to phone his club; he is not there, either. So finally she puts through the call to the house in Washington, and when she cannot find him there, she is convinced he is on his way to Lexington."

"Why didn't she take you, too?"

Mitzi pulled the peignoir more tightly about her boyish figure. "I am to stay so if Mister Baskoulos call, he will think she is still here."

"Ah, now, Mitzi! How would her husband know she had come here to my suite?"

Her penciled eyebrows arched; she shrugged one shoulder Gallic-fashion. "The same as the policemen know to come here when they do not find Madame at the Clinic, I suppose.

Mister Baskoulos, too, he knows we leave with you. One does not need to be the great detective to make inquiry at the place where you live."

"*Touché.*" He went to his bureau, took the spare belt from the top drawer. "Where will Missus Baskoulos stay, in Lexington?"

"She did not know. But I do not think she will go to the horse farm. She will call some time today to let me know."

"Where's Greld stop in Lexington? At the Old Plantation?"

"I am sorry——" she began, but his look stopped her.

"You must have heard Missus Baskoulos call him."

"Yes. But a number only; Fayette something; I do not know what it is except it is some motel." She squinted at him. "You have been hurt—your neck!"

He nodded, offering no explanation. "What's this club Mister Baskoulos belongs to?"

"Racquet and Mallet. But they do not know where he is."

He found a dark scarf, which covered the bruises on his throat and made him look like a Palm Springs playboy; he put on the belt. "When you hear from your mistress, call my office at Ambletts, let me know how to get in touch with her."

Mitzi said she would, said she was sorry . . .

He gestured impatiently, went to his closet, took the .45 he had brought back from Italy, shoved it into his pocket. "Call me if you have any word from Mister Baskoulos, too." He didn't wait for her answer, left abruptly.

Maybe, he thought, riding down with a trio of elderly female Archivists who were chattering animatedly about color microfilm—maybe Rina and Doctor Soames were on the same plane which was taking Sibyl to the Bluegrass. Lexington seemed to be the focal point; Hay-Hay Greld was there with his slick-trick agent, Sheppard Jefferson had flown there last night, Peter Baskoulos might be on his way there. But Lois

Anderson was in an ice-cold, zinc-lined box at the city morgue and Timmy Forde had one foot in the grave.

He drove past a Restaurant Grand Luxe on Forty-second Street and scowled at the early morning patrons streaming through the plate glass doors. *Choice of Gourmets from Coast to Coast.* Well, he was no connoisseur when it came to breakfast; he could take his ham and eggs without a French menu.

He had them in the Chili Grille, supplemented by the five-star finals and late city editions. The Lois Anderson murder had already been diminished in news importance by smaller headlines and briefer treatment. The "high police official" was confidently reporting "progress"—but that was all. None of the newspapers made any mention of Timmy.

Trucks from Ambletts' Long Island warehouse were just beginning to unload at the Receiving Room when he reached the Store Superlative. Wally was still on duty:

"Say, Mister Cadee, you know the conclusion I come to about that girl's bein' stabbed?"

"What, Wally?"

"She was a victim of mistake in identity, that's my opinion."

"Wouldn't be surprised if it was a question of identity." But not Lois Anderson's, he added silently. The identity of the subscriber at the phone with the two sevens and the single ought.

It was not the first time he had unlocked the Protection Office at seven-fifteen, but this morning the place seemed especially empty. Sibyl's jonquils were still on his desk, but her own colorful presence would not lighten the long day ahead.

He plugged in his outside line, put in a person-to-person to Sheppard Jefferson at the Old Plantation, Lexington, Kentucky. Then he attacked the paper work piled on his desk.

There was a memo from Andy Ryan about Sibyl's gloved

shoplifter; the booster had worn the gloves to keep salesclerks from noticing the horrid cut on the back of her left hand; a paring knife had slipped while she had been fixing supper for an invalid husband; Andy had given the girl a good talking-to and let her go.

Don penciled a V.G.J. on the memo, thinking as he did so that Sibyl also would have exercised the same "very good judgment."

His call came through.

"Figured you'd have been up for some time, watching the workouts, Mister Jefferson."

"Just back from the track a few minutes ago. What can I do for you?"

"Where does Hay-Hay Greld hang his clothes at night?"

"Why," the manager was puzzled, "at Peter's place."

"The Old Plantation? Where you are?"

"No, no. The Motel Grand Luxe, out on the Gunpowder Pike; it's run in conjunction with his restaurant here."

"Why does Greld stay at your boss's motel when they seem to be on the outs with each other?"

"They are, that's a fact." Jefferson chuckled. "I expect Hay-Hay would prefer to sack down in a stable but you don't know Charlie Daw; he gets that efficiency unit rent free and he'll keep Hay-Hay holed up there until hell's an icecap. What you want with Hay-Hay?"

"To get word to him, *pronto*."

"He won't be at the motel now; he'll be in the sweat room at the track; puts in an hour there every morning. But if it's urgent you might call the track secretary's office; he might be able to locate Charlie. Or I could run over there myself . . ."

"Be obliged if you'd do that," Don said. "Tell Greld that the young lady who's on her way down there to see him——"

"*Not Rina!*"

128

"As a matter of fact, I believe Missus Baskoulos is on a plane headed for Lexington, but——"

"You mean she's actually *left* Peter?"

"I'd say she has; they had a real blowup after you left the apartment last night."

"Oh, good God!"

"But the young lady I mentioned is Miss Forde, from my office. She's coming to find out from Greld how to get in touch with the gypsy woman he consults about his horoscopes."

"Does this have anything to do with the murder of your salesgirl?"

"Miss Forde thinks it does."

There was a "hmmmph" at the other end of the line, then a muttered expletive and—"That's the damndest thing, Mister Cadee. Charlie notified me this morning that Hay-Hay wouldn't ride *Celebrite* in the Hardboots Handicap this afternoon because he'd been warned by the stars that today is a day of doom and death. How you like that!"

"I don't," Don said. "But I would like to get word to Miss Forde that she's to call her office just as soon as possible."

"I'll give him the message," Jefferson promised. "Thing that gets me, Hay-Hay thinks *this* is the black day, not yesterday, when your clerk was killed. Would you figure that gypsy faker got her wires crossed?"

"Maybe not," said Don. "Maybe she knows something."

XX

MAYBE, DON repeated silently, as he hung up. She knows something for sure: *where Timmy Forde is*.

The call to Lexington had shown that Sib was on the right track in one respect, at least. Hay-Hay was in daily communication with his astrological adviser, must know where she could be found.

Ten minutes of telephoning produced the information that a Miss Forde had reserved a seat on Flight 112, Air-Link, turbojet, from La Guardia, destination Louisville, Kentucky . . . whence she could retrace sixty-odd miles of central Kentucky back to Lexington. E.T.A. about nine o'clock, if not too long a delay transferring to the Eastern Airlines plane for the Bluegrass.

He sent a wire, for Delivery on Disembarkation, Urgent, Special, Rush. Instructions to Western Union were long and imperative; the message to Sibyl was short and definite: CALL OFFICE IMMEDIATELY.

He phoned down to Wally at the Employees Entrance asking for Big Pat to be sent directly to the Protection Office before putting on his store uniform.

From the Confidential file he took the folder for Forde, Timothy. Not even the quarter-in-a-slot photograph could conceal the cocky grin beginning to show at the corners of

Timmy's lips or the impertinence in the boy's eyes. At the bottom of the Superior's Evaluation panel on the inside of the folder was Punctual, Alert, Energetic, but T.T.M., Personnel's cryptic abbreviation for Talks Too Much . . . wastes time chattering. Don laid the folder on his desk, photo showing, and said aloud, "I could stand hearing him say a few words, right about now."

He scowled at his watch; the second hand crawled in a snail's circle. Another hour before Sib would get his message. It was impossible to keep his mind on Inventory Loss Reports; someone in Finer Footwear had been appropriating quite a few pairs of women's thirty-dollar shoes . . . all 7B's. Well, this wouldn't be the day he would go down to Finer Footwear and inspect the feet of the salesgirls to see who wore 7B's! Recollection of the look on Lois Anderson's face when she had learned she had let the gypsy put something over made him sympathetic to salesgirls in general.

Pat showed up.

"Emergency assignment," Don told him. "Scoot over to the Mid-Broad Building. Take a notebook. Copy down the names of all tenants on the eighth, ninth, tenth and eleventh floors. Then come back here, look up the phone numbers of every tenant."

The guard scratched his chin. "I see what you're after, Mister Cadee. But you know, some of them offices in a building, people rent desk room, their names won't be on the door. Still they might have a phone."

"That's right, Pat. But I'm not looking for a fly-by-night fight promoter or a mail-a-dollar-to-Box XXX-classified-ad sharper. I'm after a number. You make out the list. I'll take it from there."

Becky came in, noticed the scarf, made the obvious inquiry about a sore throat.

He admitted it was a bit sore, let it go at that, dictated a memo to Andy Ryan, requesting her to go to Edith Forde's and stand by until he called her. He asked Becky to make a transcript of the recording wire, said there had been no progress on the Anderson murder, told her he was going down to Menswear.

The P.A. system was giving out with the morning pep-talk as he came through the aisles on the First . . . "the most valuable item in our twenty-odd million dollar inventory is invisible, intangible; it is the confidence of our customers in Ambletts—the certainty that our merchandise will prove to be exactly as represented—the assurance that neither exaggeration nor false claims is ever permitted . . ."

Frank Wilmar, haggard and hollow-eyed, was handing a ten-dollar bill to one of his girls for the floral tribute. "I'd make it fifty," he said to Don, "if I thought it would help Lois's mother to feel better. I've just been up there."

"Bad?" Don laid the twist of wool thread on the counter.

"Grandfather had a heart attack last night; they have him in the Medical Center under oxygen. Mother sits in a kind of coma holding Lois's high school graduation picture; all she'd say to me was, 'She thought the world an' all of you, Mister Wilmar; she liked everybody at Ambletts; she'd been so happy at the store.' Made me feel God-awful. I'd have gone up there last night but the police kept me downtown so late—going through those photographs."

"Do any good?"

"I think so. On the gypsy girl. Not on the chauffeur. Anyhow, that Homicide Captain is going to check my identification with people at the other stores she gypped. But I think I picked the right one; she seems to be a very dangerous criminal, a Mary Maginn."

"They know where to find her?"

Wilmar threw up his hands. "The Captain said she had no known address except the reformatory and the penitentiary.

I had no idea that anyone in this day and age actually lived on the road but that's what some of 'em do. Once in a while they'll live in a rented store for a few weeks but most of the time they're here today and in New Jersey or Pennsylvania tomorrow. What's this?"

"Thread from somebody's sleeve. Would you say it came from a man's coat or a woman's jacket?"

Wilmar reached beneath the counter, came up with a jeweler's loupe, examined the thread under the magnifying glass. "Might be either, Don. Have to take this to an expert to make sure. But offhand I'd say it's a bit of Donegal tweed. Shaggy stuff, used for high-grade sports coats, the Abercrombie sort of thing. We don't carry it in Men's suitings but they may have some of it in Mountain and Meadow, Women's Exclusive Sportswear, you could inquire."

"Yes. Thanks. I will." Don laid a five on the counter. "When is the funeral?"

"Tomorrow. At eleven." The Section Manager sighed. "You know, I couldn't get to sleep until four, trying to remember that damn phone number. It's going to drive me to a psychiatrist if the police don't find that gypsy girl."

"Just a question of time, Frank." That's all, he told himself irritably; just a question of fifteen hours to that appointment for Sibyl at Grand Luxe Commissary #7.

Dooley was at the water cooler by the Confidential files when Don got back to the office. The Captain was caustic:

"You're a hard man to get along with, Cadee. You tell me you're taking Baskoulos' wife to the hospital; instead you run her around to your hotel."

"Lady refused to go to a hospital. I'd say the reason is she's pregnant and doesn't want her husband to know about it."

"See? That's what I mean. You pick up information I can use and clam up on me." Dooley eyed the scarf thoughtfully. "Like you knew about that location of Madame Marbola's down on Harkover Street, but I have to dig it out of Missus Baskoulos instead of getting it from you."

"That gyp joint was where Ambletts' credit coin was stolen, Captain. If there's anything that ties up Marbola with the Anderson girl's murder, I haven't heard about it."

Dooley picked up a brief case from the base of the water cooler. "That pair of men's shorts, you heard about that, you saw it. And there's this." He drew out a six-by-ten glossy print of a dark-haired young woman who would have been strikingly handsome if she had not worn such a sullen expression; her eyes were hostile, there was a suggestion of a sneer at her nostrils. "Your Section Manager put the finger on her last night. Mary Maginn, with as many aliases as a jailful of shoplifters and—take a peek at her record."

Pasted on the back of the photo was a typed sheet:

Maginn, Mary, 24, 138#, 5'5", olive complexion, eyes black, hair black, lips full, ears small-pointed, nose aquiline, teeth regular, no facial blemishes, mole on left shoulder.
Confidence worker.
Arrested 6/27/55, Newark, N.J. Grand larceny. Complaining witness refused testimony at trial, apparently terrified at sight of M. Maginn.
Arrested 10/2/55, Scranton, Pa. Grand theft, convicted, sentenced 2–5, suspended on partial repayment to victimized elderly woman.
Arrested 11/24/56, Modesto, Cal. Jumped bail $2000, indictment pending.
Arrested 2/9/57, Miami, Fla. Conspiracy to extort. Charges amended to include atrocious assault with intent to murder arresting officer, stabbed six times with ice pick. Served 6 months, Fla. State Penitentiary, paroled.
Note: This woman is extremely dangerous when facing apprehension; flies into a fury of slashing with broken glass or any sharp, pointed instrument. Notify Chief, Police Department, Modesto, Cal.

"I see what you mean," Don said slowly. " 'Any sharp, pointed instrument' could have been a surgeon's scalpel."

"That's what I'm going to tell the Grand Jury this afternoon. You'll be getting a subpoena to appear, too. You'll be asked about this kidnaping of your stock boy, but that's not down my alley, except insofar as the kid's abductor may also be the girl's murderer. I'm going up to your hotel to get Missus Baskoulos to verify Wilmar's identification of Mary Maginn."

"Save yourself a trip, Captain. The lady's left town."

Dooley paused midway in the process of replacing the photo in his brief case. "Where'd she go?"

"Lexington, Kentucky."

"Why?"

"She's afraid her husband's fixing to kill her lover."

The Captain looked as if he'd bitten into an apple and had discovered half a worm. "Baskoulos gone to Kentucky, too?"

"Don't know," Don said. "Haven't been able to locate him at his apartment or his club. But I do have reason to believe that the gypsy hellcat has gone to Lexington, too."

The Captain stared. "If you're not trying to sidetrack me again . . ."

"No."

"Then I'll notify the Lexington police about Mary."

"Damn good idea," Don agreed. "And you might throw in a warning about Peter Baskoulos. I have a feeling that somebody down in Lexington is going to get badly hurt."

XXI

FIVE MINUTES past nine. Down on the First floor the early patrons would be sauntering in through the hallowed portals of the cathedral of fashion. Salesgirls would be excitedly gossiping about Lois Anderson. Five past nine; no word from Sibyl.

He would wait another half-hour; planes could be delayed by fog or head winds.

He made out a check, thinking, here goes the down payment on the cottage on the not too secluded lake in Connecticut. Maybe you ought to put it up to Bob Stolz, have Ambletts advance the cash. No, if the ransom deal went through and the merchandise was recovered, Protex would pay off and Don would get his money back. If it didn't go through—then the money wouldn't matter; Edith Forde would never get Timmy back.

Don went to the Luggage Section, borrowed a lightweight suitcase, took it to Cashiers. The girls at the pay-roll machines made a noble effort to restrain their curiosity as he stacked packets of ones and fives in the one-suiter.

Nine-thirty. Still no call from Sib—but a peremptory one from Bob Stolz.

Becky said: "Charlotte says the hurricane warnings are flying, Mister Cadee."

"Vortex coming closer all the time, yes." He sat the suitcase beside his desk. "Check on that Eastern Airlines plane, find out if it's landed at Lexington. If Sibyl calls, transfer it to Mister Stolz's office."

It was not difficult to anticipate what Bob would have to say: let the police handle the homicide, let the FBI take over on Timmy. Reasonable enough, still Don couldn't do it; he had a personal responsibility in both cases. He'd have to turn in his resignation if Bob insisted on a hands-off policy.

Charlotte murmured: "Stand by for heavy weather. Go right in."

Stolz didn't even say "Good morning." He hammered a fist on a blue-backed legal paper lying on his blotter. "Summons to appear as defendants in a civil action for one hundred thousand dollars' damages! Filed by Peter Baskoulos this morning against Ambletts and its Protection Chief!"

"On what grounds?" asked Don.

"Theft of personal property, willful retention of same! One spool of recording wire, forcibly removed from plaintiff's home. You do that?"

"Yep. Not as Ambletts' representative, though—as an individual. But I wouldn't concede that what was on the wire was Baskoulos' property. I'm having a transcript of it made right now; I'll have it sent up with the spool—you can turn it over to your Greek friend any time you want to, after you've read what's on it."

Stolz banged his fist on the summons again. "Don't call that bastard my friend. He spent half an hour on the phone early this morning, offering to withdraw the suit if I'd fire you."

"I'll make it easy for you, Bob. I quit."

"*Hell you do!*" Stolz swore. "Ambletts will go a long way to play ball with its customers, but I'm a son of a bitch if I let anybody tell us who to keep on our payroll; I told him so. He came back at me by threatening to press criminal charges against you."

"For socking him in the jaw?" Why, bless the boss's surly ol' soul—for once he's not backing down in the face of a patron's wrath, he's backing you up!

"Said the warrant would charge atrocious assault." Stolz permitted himself a wry grin. "Did you really belt him out? He was a light-heavy champ in college, you know."

"I caught him off guard; he was trying to kill his wife."

The General Manager of the Store Superlative scowled darkly. "Funny. From what he bellowed over the phone I gathered that what actually got under his skin was that you'd put the police up to giving him a hard time about the Anderson girl's death. Said you'd found someone, at this office building where she was murdered, to identify him as having been there at the time she was stabbed, when as a matter of fact he'd been at the Racquet and Mallet with Shep Jefferson, manager of his stables."

"He gave himself a hard time, Bob—by telling off those Homicide boys."

"He would. That's his temperament, he's a Tell-off Boy. But why would he get sore about a possible accusation in the matter of the Anderson's girl's murder when he knew you could counter by showing he'd tried to kill Rina?"

"He didn't believe his wife would testify against him, figured that she'd offset what I would say. But Brother B. was wrong; she's left him; she'll not only testify against him, she might take more direct action. You'll see what I mean when you read that transcript."

"Did Peter have anything to do with our employee's murder, in your opinion?"

"Don't know, Bob. Trying to find out."

"Um." Stolz was not happy. "Cop job, isn't it? Don't go out of your way to antagonize Peter. Let me handle that end of it. You haven't been served with the warrant yet?"

"No."

"Then stay out of the store until I can try to talk some sense into him through his lawyers. If it gets to the point where we have to go your bail on a criminal charge, he'll never drop it until the whole mess of dirty linen has been laundered in court; he's that sort. So take the day off while I block that charge, go fishing or something."

"It's a little early in the season," Don said, "but I might go hunting, instead."

"For the Forde kid? No word from him yet?"

"We've heard from him, Bob. He phoned Sibyl last night. We expect him home tonight. I'll keep you in touch . . ." If you tell Stolz about the ransom note, he may pick up the phone and yell for the federals; that could really tear it. Important thing was to get Sibyl back to New York in time to keep that ransom rendezvous.

Ten to ten when he got back to the Protection Office. Becky had baffling news. The Louisville-to-Lexington plane had arrived on time; the airport had paged Miss Forde but apparently she had not been aboard.

"Call Hayworth Greld at the Motel Grand Luxe, Lexington." Don fumed. "And if anybody shows up with a summons or a warrant or a subpoena—I'm out of town for the day."

He waited in his office for fifteen minutes before Becky signaled on the intercom. "DNA on Mister Greld; I left the call in but they seem to think that if he did not answer the first time he must be at the track for the day. I'd have called in earlier only there was a sour-looking specimen here asking for you and he wouldn't state his business so I waited until he went away. Shall I try to get Mister Greld at the race track?"

"No." Even if Sibyl had somehow not heard her name being called as she left the plane, there had been plenty of time for Shep Jefferson to have spoken to Hay-Hay and passed along the urgent message to call the office. Something had gone wrong. *If you're going hunting, you'd better head for*

Lexington. "See what's the earliest reservation you can get on a plane to Lexington."

It took half an hour to get the bad news. The first available seat on a flight to the Bluegrass would be the six o'clock from La Guardia. Another quarter-hour to talk to the charter plane service at Newark and arrange for a twin-motored four-place Grumman to be on the strip when Don reached there.

He asked Becky to get the recording transcript to Stolz, to get the list of phone numbers from Pat, to let Andy know he would call her at Edith's later. It was exactly eleven when he tossed the suitcaseful of cash into a taxi at the side entrance; twenty to twelve when he reached Newark Airport.

The pilot of the twin-motor job was a youth who must have been in rompers about the time Don had learned geography the hard way in the Pacific, but the young man was adult enough to recognize that his charter passenger was not in a conversational mood. He introduced himself briefly, confined himself to getting the most out of the Grumman.

The drone of the motors, plus the strain of waiting, added to his lack of sleep the night before, made Don bone-weary. Just before he fell asleep, with the serpentine Delaware glittering in bright sunlight far below, he recalled his first experience with gypsies . . .

It had been at the Danbury Fair, one Saturday night in the early fall; he must have been fifteen, full of fizz and vinegar, with a dollar or so to spend on Roll-a-Ball or the Wheel of Fortune . . . but he had ventured the dollar to have his palm read by a voluptuous creature in a red and yellow blouse, very loose in front and cut very low. The gypsy had dropped a fortunetelling card on the dirt floor of the tent with the big black palm on the oilcloth banner; she had bent over to pick it up; the blouse had disclosed tantalizing charms; she had noticed his gawky interest, had winked . . .

Once the dollar had been handed over, however, the come-on smile vanished, the reading of his past and future was hasty and annoyingly trite. He had felt sheepish at having been cozened into spending his money, had formed his opinion of all gypsies then and there.

But as he fell into a doze, he dreamed that he was back in that dark and odorous tent, sitting at the little card table with his hand foolishly held out for the fake perusal. But it was not the girl who was opposite him; it was Yosef Maginn. And he was saying:

"Your name is Cadee."

Even in a dream, Don wondered: How had Yosef known him, known his name? Who had given the gypsy the description of Ambletts' Protection Chief?

He had the feeling it might be all-important to know the answer.

XXII

HE SLEPT until the plane lost altitude over the gently rolling hills of the Bluegrass, the fields platted in shades of green and brown, grass-green, corn-green, panels of white cheesecloth over young tobacco, the brown of newly seeded fields. It was quarter past four in the land of the long white fences.

"Top off your tanks; get set for a fast take-off," he told the pilot after the smooth landing. "I'll just leave my suitcase here, in the plane."

The Keeneland track was only minutes away, across the Versailles pike; he rolled up to the admission gate just as a roar erupted from the grandstand—the "They're *off!*" for the start of the sixth.

He reached the Racing Secretary's office amid the pandemonium of a neck-and-neck finish. The girl in the Secretary's office suggested that Jockey Greld would probably be in the paddock; certainly his agent, Mister Daw, would be there to watch the saddling of *Findingo*, the Old Plantation entry in the seventh race. "He's a short, squatty little man; he'll be wearing a white, ten-gallon, Texas hat."

The crowd milling about the pari-mutuel windows began to stream back to their seats in clubhouse or grandstand; automatically Don looked for Sibyl among the smartly dressed women, knowing well she wouldn't be watching the races or betting on them.

Late afternoon sunlight filtered through the trees around the paddock, dappling the slowly circling horses with flecks of glossy copper, freckling the oversized Stetson on a short man with a face which seemed to have lost a head-on argument with a truck. He regarded Don with sullen hostility at the latter's "You Charlie Daw?"

"If you're tryin' to collect dough, no."

"I'm trying to get in touch with Hay-Hay Greld. Did Mister Jefferson get a message through to your boy?"

"Your name Cadee?"

"Right."

"Do me a favor. Have a helping of arsenic. Drop dead." The agent had eyes which reminded Don of fat green worms. "You need any help, I'll be gladda lend a hand."

"I can appreciate the fact that you have troubles of your own but——"

"But nuts! Shep says your gal wants to ask my boy how to contact the witch-bitch; that's all we need, he should get some more curdling from that star-gazin' stupe. You know what she done? She cost him a cut of the purse on *Celebrite* in the fifth an' maybe a slice of the seventh because he won't put a boot in the stirrup today. She fixed us, that's what she done with that crack she made last night—an' if she don't lay off him I'm gonna make mash potatoes out of what's in her skull, I'm not kiddin', mister."

"What crack was that?"

Charlie Daw poked a stiffened forefinger at Don's Adam's apple; the fat green worms showed through a fierce squint. "She should cast up them horoscopes strictly for horses; they couldn't be affected—instead of scaring my boy outa the saddle with such mucking prognossications. 'This is a day of dark and dreadful deeds,' says this gypsy dipsy-doodle, 'a merchant of murder will bargain for your heart's blood, take no chances today.' So the dumbhead won't put a leg up on a couple cinch winners; he's sulkin' in his tent an' my commission is no per cent of nothin'."

"We ought to team up," Don said. "I'm as anxious as you are to put this female astrologer out of business. She stole a raft of merchandise from my department store; the police are after her. Help me locate her; maybe we can get her off your neck."

"Take five, pal." Daw held out his hand. "I'm with you. But you'll have to shoot your own film, see what develops. I got no more idea how Hay-Hay hooks up with this doomsday dame then how to get a broken-down nag in orbit. I try to keep an eye on him, but he sneaks out when I grab a spot of snooze, uses some pay booth to ring her up."

"First thing is to find Miss Forde. Did you pass on my message to Hay-Hay?"

"Yeh, yeh. One'll get you the daily double if she gets him to utter peep A about that zodiac-zombie. But you could fret up a sweat in the steam room, ask him."

"Where do I find it? All right for me to stalk right in?"

"They ain't gonna mistake you for no disbarred jock. Go to that building, second door on the right. But it won't do no good to mention your talk to me; we practically have a knockdown an' kick-in-the-teeth this noon when he wantsta slide back to the motel. Our contract calls for him to show up in silks every race day whether he weighs in or not so I ain't gonna heave *that* hundred bucks out th' window."

"Did Jefferson tell you Missus Baskoulos is in town?"

"Yeh, yeh. Her I don't mind so bad; she don't try to run my boy durin' racing hours. It's this long-distance hocus-pocus has me cuttin' up paper horses. You go on, see what you can squeeze out of a dried prune; I'll see y' here, after."

"*The horses are beginning the parade to the post*," announced the paddock speaker as Don strode into the misty heat of the steam room. Naked men, muscular and big-

144

shouldered but no larger than twelve-year-old boys, lay on canvas bunks, played checkers, read comic books, watched TV. None paid any heed to the man from Ambletts until he inquired of one naked gnome watching the baseball game on the screen of the portable: "Which one is Greld?"

The gnome gazed around the room. "None of 'em. He ain't here."

One of the checker players spoke without looking up from the board. "He left, hour ago. King me, podner, king me."

Don went out into the cool, fresh air, mopped his dripping face. Left without telling Daw? Or had the agent been slipping over a fast one?

When Don got back to the paddock, Charlie Daw wasn't around. Nor could Don locate him in the excited crowd yelling its favorites on in the stretch drive of the seventh race.

He would have used a phone to call up the Motel Grande Luxe, but there were no public phones at race-tracks. He settled for a cab, gave the driver the sketchy address—out on the Gunpowder Pike.

"Mister," said the taximan, "don't worry about not knowing the number. That Grand Luxe deal is about as well known now as the Lafayette Hotel; I mean, man, that's a heavy-doin' operation. De Luxe and de-lovely."

The motel was a huge semicircle of seventy units behind southern colonial white pillars; the red rotunda of the restaurant building's hemisphere was set off by a dozen more of the chaste white columns. There must have been fifty cars lined up at the two buildings—a handsome tribute to the success of Peter Baskoulos.

Don held out a five. "Have a sandwich, bottle of beer; I may be a few minutes."

"It would upset my stomach to pay a buck and a quarter for a hamburg," the driver said, "but I'll hit you for the beer. Beep the horn when you're ready to roll."

145

At the office a genial young man glanced at his key rack. "Mister Greld? In 61, but I don't think he's there; seems to me a young lady was inquiring for him an hour or so ago and I couldn't get him on his telephone. But I'll try him now——"

"Don't bother," Don called over his shoulder. "I just dropped by for a minute, anyway."

There was no car in the parking slot in front of 61. The Venetian blinds were down all the way and closed tightly.

A young lady . . . inquiring for him. Sib?

He knocked at the door of 61.

He waited, knocked again, reached for the brass doorknob to see if the door was locked, felt something sticky, withdrew his hand, looked at his fingers.

Blood. Fresh blood.

XXIII

DURING THE ten seconds which it took him to whip out his handkerchief and wipe, first the knob to remove his fingerprints, then his blood-smeared hand, fear poured over him like crushing surf. Sibyl had come to Lexington to find Hay-Hay Greld; she would have found out he lived here at Baskoulos' Motel Grand Luxe. Had she come here? *Was she still here?*

Don tried the knob again; it turned. He glanced around at an Italian sports car which had rolled up to 64 with a young couple; they were too intent on each other—honeymooners, possibly, he guessed—to pay any attention to him. He went in quickly—felt a surge of relief that there was no corpse stretched on the wall-to-wall carpet.

He stepped to the bathroom door; no one behind that shower curtain. The closet adjoining was full of clothes, sports jackets on hangers, bathrobes and pajamas—all masculine gender. He scanned the room swiftly.

Twin beds, candlewick covers unmussed. On the bed-table by the right-hand twin, a pile of *Morning Telegraphs*, some *Turf and Sports Digests*, topped by a trio of plastic pill phials. On the other bed-table, a stack of astrological magazines. Piles more of the horoscopic journals heaped by the bed along with bundles of *Day by Day With Your Lucky Star*, shoe boxes full of fortunetelling cards, *Find Your Own Fate Scien-*

tifically charts, a welter of numerology pamphlets, lucky charms, amulets, rabbits' feet mounted in ivory, silver, gold. There in the corner was the trunk Sibyl had said the jockey used as his portable library shelves.

But then why was the library itself strewn all about the room? Don hefted the trunk; it was heavy; it was unlocked; he swung up the lid.

She lay on her side with her knees doubled up against her stomach, her head bent forward in the cramped space so that her hair, smooth and satiny as black glass, rested on the scarlet-stained bath towel which had been stuffed beneath her body. She had not been dead many minutes for the olive skin of her face was still warm and the eyeballs had not begun to recede in the sockets.

If he had not recognized her from the photograph, he would have done so by reason of the swanky Bahama Sand suit, the shirtmaker blouse, the chain of heavy gold coins, which her murderer had not bothered to remove.

Madame Marbola. He wondered whether she herself had found "Peace of Mind" at last, after such an unpeaceful end. She, too, had been stabbed in the back; this "Merchant of Murder" traded in treacherous attacks . . . on women and children. This latest meant that Sibyl's trip had been in vain; there would be no information now from Mary Maginn.

Don did not lift the body or turn it to examine the wound; he had little doubt the coroner's verdict would be that the fatal blow had been struck with a small, thin blade—like a surgeon's knife. But he did remove the ostrich handbag—the duplicate of the one Rina Baskoulos had "lost."

He emptied its contents on the bed which must have been Charlie Daw's. A roll of bills; not a large roll and, from quick inspection, nothing bigger than twenties. Small suede purse with credit coins from Ambletts and three other stores; he put the purse in his pocket. Pack of filter-tips, ring of keys, box of safety matches, tiny skull carved out of ivory, peanut-brittle bar, compact set with imitation rubies, folded map of Fayette County, Kentucky, eyelash make-up, small bottle of aspirin, miniature deck of playing cards, nail file, lipstick, and a black card such as Rina had found in her elevator. But there was nothing about the Priestess of Peace of Mind, only a row of cabalistic letters crudely printed in white ink:

YM.TTTT.TO.VETRPET.RD.TVIL.SI.

He was wondering what sort of cipher it might be, when the door opened softly.

A short, bowlegged young man, with the lined and leathery face of an aged farmer; the blue eyes curiously bright in sunken sockets. His ears were too large, his nose was too snubby, his mouth was too wide; he was almost a caricature of the homely man—but there was no mistaking the vitality in those piercingly sharp eyes.

He said nothing until he had surveyed the room, spotted the confusion of horoscopic literature. His glance flashed to the open trunk. "Why you goddam!"—he closed the door, came toward Don with the mincing step of a dog walking on glare ice. He saw the dead gypsy, dropped to his haunches beside the trunk.

Don said: "I came here looking for you, Greld. Somebody smeared blood on your doorknob, making a getaway after killing your friend, there. Door was open, so I came in——"

His explanation was cut short by the jockey's half-strangled cry of anguish, by a lightning-fast lunge, by powerful forearms which caught Don behind the knees, jerked his legs out from beneath him.

His head hit the corner of the trunk at the same split second Greld butted him savagely in the stomach, knocking the

149

wind out of him. Flat on his back, he saw the boot heel stamping down at his mouth, rolled aside reflexively. The heel landed on his neck. He tried to twist away from the next stamping.

"You won't get any chance"—heel on the shoulder—"to hire some slick lawyer"—kick in the ear—"get off with some lousy ten years"—boot in the groin—"you won't even go to jail—"

Don grabbed an ankle, pulled the jockey down on top of him. Fists flailed at his teeth, his eyes . . . but fists were not as lethal as those hard, leather heels.

"You killed the one real friend"—Greld panted—"I got in the whole world"—he back-elbowed Don on the point of the jaw—"I'm not even gonna let you get to the hospital"—he got his strong fingers around Don's throat.

Don tried a "bridge" remembered from his college wrestling matches; he used his knee, street-fighting style; he got his fingers in Greld's hair and tore out a handful. But the grip at his windpipe did not relax.

If you can't knock him loose from his senses in the next ten seconds—Don was surprised to discover how calmly he could analyze the struggle with this pint-size fury—*who will get that ransom to Commissary #7 in time to save Timmy?*

Suddenly the unbearable pressure relaxed. Greld screeched like a wounded bobcat, sprang to his feet spitting curses. "You damn near put my eye out with your goddam cigarette!"

The nasal voice of the jockey's agent came to Don like the hoofbeats of U. S. Cavalry horses in old Western movies. "I woulda shoved the live butt right up ya crummy nose to save you from committin' a murder. Or maybe I was too late, anyways? You got a slow leak in ya brain?"

Greld howled: "*He* done it, Charlie. I come in while he's stuffin' her in th' trunk. The one true friend I got."

"What am I? A nennamy?" Daw demanded.

Don managed to growl: "The gypsy was dead when I got here; chances are she'd been dead twenty minutes, maybe half an hour. At the time she must have been stabbed, I was in the jockey room at Keeneland, looking for you, Greld."

The jockey crawled on hands and knees to the trunk, put his hand reverently on Mary Maginn's hair, stroking it gently.

"Cadee's right." Charlie Daw held out a hand to help Don to his feet. "An' you're wrong, like so often. First you lie to me about stayin' in the steam room until the weigh-in for the eighth. Then you run out on me. Now, to catch the climax, you must of had a date with this crystal-gazin' chick—so now what do we do? Put an ad in the *Bloodline?* Have corpse, will travel?"

Don said: "Keep your boy under control; I'll go speak to the management."

The agent snarled: "Cops I need like a hole in the haircut. Who coulda got in our bunkhouse without your key, Hay-Hay? You give that key to anybody?"

"To Madame Marbola," Greld admitted. "She came to the jock house, sent in a message. I get one of the valets to take the key out to her, tell her I'll meet her here around five."

"So who else," Daw moaned, holding the brim of his ten-gallon hat in despair, "who knows she's gonna be here? Who wants to keep her from cozyin' up to you? Missus Boss-Baskoulos, hah?"

Don went to the door. "I wouldn't touch that stuff that came out of her handbag. Police will want to go over that." All, he told himself as he stepped out into the cool of the April afternoon, except the little black card with the cryptic lettering. That might be the only chance left . . . for Timmy.

At the office he spoke again to the affable manager. "You give anyone a passkey to let 'em in Number 61 this afternoon?"

"No," the day clerk said. "We don't give passkeys to anyone except the maids." He hesitated. "Was there any trouble? Mister Baskoulos was around, an hour or so ago . . . he has passkeys to all his properties, of course."

XXIV

DON WASN'T too surprised that the Greek was in Kentucky; if Baskoulos had suspected that his wife had come to Lexington, it would have been the restaurant man's way to try to trap her with the jockey. But it was a shock to consider the possibility that Baskoulos had murdered the gypsy. The only plausible inference was that, if he had killed her, it must have been because he had conspired with her in tricking Rina. But it wasn't conceivable the millionaire would be involved in the kidnaping of Timmy Forde; what big operator would mess around with a five thousand dollar ransom!

"You're outside city limits, aren't you?" he asked the motel clerk.

"Mile over the line. Why?"

"Better ring your state trooper barracks," Don said.

"What's happened?" The clerk was agitated. "Somebody hurt?" He turned to the switchboard, plugged in.

"That is——" Don was about to add "an understatement," but through the office picture window he saw a long, black limousine swing in fast off the pike to the arc by the motel units; the tires were still scattering gravel when what seemed, at first glance, to be a little old lady in a black shawl began to climb out. But the little old lady carried an ostrich leather bag; she had blonde hair, not gray. Don finished with "—exactly right. Someone *has* been hurt." He went out quickly.

A Negro in a violet silken jacket slashed with hoops of bright orange descended hastily from the driver's seat to help Rina Baskoulos.

Don whistled. The Negro turned. Don shook his head in pantomime. The servant paused.

Rina spoke crossly: "What's wrong with you, Emory!"

Don got close enough to speak without shouting: "Wouldn't go in there, now."

"Mister Cadee!" She frowned accusingly. "You trailed me down here from New York!"

"Not at all. No." He noticed the pallor of the flawless skin, the swathing of bandages beneath the shawl. "Matter of fact, I flew down to find my assistant at the store." He took her arm, gently, as she moved toward 61. "She came to Lexington to see Greld, too—but this isn't the right time for either of you to talk to him."

Rina said: "Why?"

"State troopers will be here in a few minutes. Only make things more difficult all around for you to have to explain your presence while the police are making inquiries about a murder."

"*Here?*"

"Yes. Just now." He urged her back toward the car.

"Oh no! Oh NO!" She tried to break loose.

"Madame Marbola. Stabbed to death."

Rina gazed at him blankly for a moment, as if she did not understand. "*Marbola!*" Then she put her palms together in an attitude of grateful prayer. "Dear God!" She opened her eyes. "I thought . . . Peter had been here."

"He has been," Don said. "Not in there now, though."

"If Hayworth is in trouble over that frightful woman," Rina became excited, "I must be with him; I must."

154

"Daw is with him. You'd only make matters worse." Don saw the motel clerk run out of the office toward Unit 61. "Get back in your car before——"

The clerk saw the limousine, swerved, halted: "Missus Baskoulos, you know where I can find Mister Baskoulos?"

"I wish I did," Rina said tightly.

The motel man eyed Don with open suspicion. "If you do happen to run across him, he's needed here." He hurried on to Greld's unit.

Don half lifted the blonde into the rear seat of the limousine: "Get going!" he ordered the servant in the Baskoulos colors.

"Back to the hotel, Miz Rina?" asked the driver.

"The Old Plantation, Emory." She sank back, exhausted. "I don't seem to have much freedom of action when Mister Cadee is around. So let's take him to the young lady he's trying to locate—perhaps he'll let me alone then."

"Miss Forde's at your farm?" Don's relief at pulling away from Motel Grand Luxe before the arrival of a state police squad was nothing compared to that resulting from knowing where Sibyl was.

"She is. When I got to the Lafayette I called the motel, but Hayworth wasn't in. So I rang up the Plantation, got Shep. He told me Hayworth wasn't there—he sometimes does go out to our exercise track when he's not racing—but a young lady from Ambletts was there, looking for him."

A tan car, with POLICE in large black letters on its sides roared past with siren squealing. "What made her think Greld might be at the farm?" Don asked.

"Shep said Charlie Daw told her Hayworth had gone out there. What worried me was, he also said your Miss Forde was having a terrific argument with Peter—and that was the first I knew that Peter was actually in Kentucky, though of course I'd been afraid of it because he had threatened so many times to kill Hayworth. That's why I came down, when Doctor Soames insisted I was much too ill to travel."

A terrific argument? What was that about? Lois? Timmy? Don said: "You came down to kill your husband."

The limousine swung off the wide cement of the Gunpowder Pike, onto a narrow winding blacktop bordered by the whitewashed rail fences of the horse farms, lush emerald fields, impressive gateways. *Why would anyone who could afford a horse farm in this rich country bother with a ransom that wouldn't pay for one of those rollicking colts?*

"I did." She tapped the ostrich handbag. "One of the things that delayed me after reaching the hotel here was arranging to buy the pistol I have in here. You have no idea how difficult it is for a woman to buy a gun over the telephone; of course I couldn't ask the doctor to buy it for me; he doesn't know I have it or what I mean to do with it."

"Another good murder is just what we need," Don said bleakly.

"This will be a good one," she answered wearily. "It will save the man I love and the child I will bear him; it may well save my own life. I am prepared to pay whatever penalty may be demanded. Peter has abused me both publicly and privately; he has hurt me and tried to burn me to death, I would have left him months ago, when Hayworth and I fell in love, except that I had been brought up in a faith which holds the marriage bond an unbreakable one. Of course that bond was actually broken long ago, right after our marriage, when I knew I could never love such a man." She pointed to the red brick mansion which appeared from behind a screen of stately oaks set far back from the winding road. "The Old Plantation; it's beautiful, isn't it? Sad and beautiful, that so much hate and savage ugliness should live in a place like that."

The limousine paused for Emory to pull the rope at the horse-gate.

"Better give me that gun," Don said.

"Don't worry; I shan't shoot Peter while you're around."

"No need of fireworks at all, Missus Baskoulos. Greld will be in the custody of the state police; your husband won't be able to carry out his threat. I don't mean to let you go through with yours." She made a show of resistance but he took the bag away, opened it, put the stubby, nickeled hammerless in his pocket. "Where is Doctor Soames?"

"At the track. I told him I would meet him there, in Peter's box—that was the only way I could get him to leave me." She leaned forward. "The office, Emory. I don't want to go to the house . . . yet."

The limousine rolled past the rose-brick of the great house, circled a garage, stopped before a small white cottage. Sheppard Jefferson, in shirt sleeves and a yellowed panama, came out to the low porch; his long, narrow face was gray with strain. He said "Hello" to Don; to Rina he said: "I wish to God you'd brought that doctor along; he could at least give me a shot if Peter wouldn't let him prescribe for him. For the first time since I've known him, I'm afraid of him, Rina. He's gone berserk."

Don said: "Where's Miss Forde?"

"I left them over at the south barn; Peter went to look at *Politure*, the horse we just brought over from Ireland to stand at stud here." The manager helped Rina to a chair in the office, which was like a living room with file cases. "He's going to sue the syndicate that paid the three hundred thousand for *Politure*, that's his latest lunacy. Isn't enough that he's suing Ambletts for damages, you for assault, Mister Cadee; Rina for divorce, and Hay for alienation." He lit a cigarette with a hand that was none too steady. "Wouldn't surprise me one bit if he sued Miss Forde for trespass or mopery or something. He did tell her to get the hell off the place; told her it was lucky she's a girl or he'd have thrown her off, bodily. I'm not exaggerating, Rina—I think Peter's gone loco."

"Where," said Don grimly, "is this south barn?"

Emory said, "I take you there right fast. Jus' hop in."

XXV

THE LIMOUSINE drew up at a brown, dirt oval—a cooling-out ring. Beyond, the wide-open, hip-roofed barn exhaled into the shadowy dusk an agreeable smell of hay and horse. A trio of coveralled Negroes squatted on upturned feed tubs; on the dirt before them a portable radio blatted:

". . . crossed up faithful followers of the orange and violet by a last minute substitution of Sonny Kupchek for its top banana, Hay-Hay Greld, in the rich Phoenix Stakes. Sonny did his best, no doubt, but compared to the tough little jock they call 'The Most,' Sonny sat very small in the saddle as the Old Plantation entry finished a bad, sad fifth. Now the question is——"

One of the grooms turned down the volume as Don got out.

The question, Don repeated to himself, *is why Charlie Daw sent Sibyl to the horse farm, knowing Greld would not be here.* "Where'll I find Peter Baskoulos?"

The grooms exchanged impassive glances.

After a pause, the oldest gestured toward the barn, dead-pan. "The boss in there. Was it me, I would not care to disturb him, unless it's on a urgent matter; he don't seem to be in the mood for welcoming strangers."

Another added solemnly: "He like to bit my head off for jus' passin' the time of day."

Emory said: "Gentleman's looking for a young lady came to see Mister Baskoulos—you seen her?"

"Yeah, boy," answered the third groom, "*and* heard her. She start disputin' with the boss right smart but I guess he sent her a-scootin' and a-flyin'—been all quiet in there, last half hour."

The eldest nodded. "Boss in there with a good-lookin' gal, we stay put; none of our business is it feudin', a-fussin' or a-fightin'.'"

Emory raced his motor. "She must of gone back to the big house; I'll run you right over."

"Wait." Don stalked to the barn. "Hold it a minute." He didn't like that "all quiet in there"; his experience with Baskoulos had been that the Greek was anything but a silent man. Still, except for the gentle nickering from one of the stalls or the nervous stamp of a heavy foot, it *was* all quiet.

Behind him, the motor raced impatiently. Soft laughter was cut short by Emory's sharp reprimand.

If Sibyl had gone back to the mansion, why hadn't Shep Jefferson known it? If she hadn't—if she was still here——

"Sib," he called. "Oh, Sibyl."

From the stall to his right came a loud whinny; a jet-black head turned inquiringly. Don saw the name on the varnished board, called: "All right, *Merry Lea*, wasn't talking to you . . ."

What was it Shep Jefferson had said: Baskoulos had gone to look at his newly imported Irish stud horse?

He scanned the stall-boards on each side. *Basky Boy, Samatan, Bull Runner, Findingo, Tax Return* . . .

"Sibyl!"

Baskoulos must have gone back, too; he'd have heard Don, recognized the Protection man's voice.

Gilly Gal, Do Bettor . . . there—*Politure!*

He spoke the stallion's name aloud. Gray ears twitched

irritably, a long, bony nose showed flaring nostrils; the big horse drew its lips back threateningly.

"Now, now . . . take it easy——"

The stallion reared. A forehoof glistened in the dim light.

Don stepped to the door of the stall. In the pool of shadow behind the animal, close to the hind hoofs, crumpled loosely like a pile of old clothes tossed carelessly on the floor, lay the restaurant magnate. His face was a gory smear; his black hair was matted to his crushed-in forehead; all that could be actually seen of the once-handsome face was a hideous grin, the teeth bared in a sickening resemblance to those of the menacing stallion.

There was something in the Greek's right hand. Don knelt to see what it was.

A siren split the silence, mounted to a piercing crescendo; headlights threw a brightening loom into the gloomy cavern of the barn.

The thing in Baskoulos' death grip was a knife; a thin bright blade about six inches long, no more than half the width of a paring knife.

The siren wailed to a stop out by the limousine.

State troopers, directed to the Old Plantation by that motel clerk who had seen Don drive away with Rina Baskoulos. The officers would have heard from Charlie Daw and Hay-Hay that Don had been in Greld's motel room with the dead gypsy. It might be possible to explain that away, but how much chance would he have to keep out of custody when they found him with the body of Peter Baskoulos?

A check with the New York police would bring out the fact that Don had fought with the Greek in the Baskoulos apartment last night. That he had subsequently taken Peter's wife to his own hotel suite. That, obviously, he had followed Baskoulos to the Bluegrass and had there met the Greek's wife once more, had driven away with her.

You may be able to clear yourself in spite of the incriminating circumstances, but they won't let you loose until you do clear things up: that'll take a while. Meantime, what about Timmy Forde? Who'll keep that ransom date—and with what? It's nearly seven now; if they hold you up even a couple of hours, you'll never get Sibyl back to Commissary #7 in time to beat the deadline.

Lights flashed on, the length of the barn. *Those tough state cops will likely take a shot at you, if they think you're trying to give them the slip. But there's nothing else to do.*

Thirty or forty feet away were the big doors at the far end of the barn. He ran, ignoring shouted commands behind him.

The doors were unlocked. He reached them as a warning shot echoed through the stall area.

He got through, took five seconds to shut the doors, sprinted through the gloom toward the lighted windows of the mansion a quarter-mile away.

One thing sure, he couldn't leave without Sibyl; the writer of the ransom note had been explicit on that—she was the only one the kidnapers would trust.

What if she had already left the Old Plantation? How was he to locate her in time to make the flight back? And if she was still here at the horse farm, the police might give her a bad time after learning she'd been the last one known to have been with the Greek.

He circled behind a tractor shed, cut in between a small stone building, which he supposed was an old smokehouse, and the Plantation office, now brightly lighted. Neither Shep Jefferson nor Rina Baskoulos was visible.

What had happened back there in *Politure's* stall? Was it possible that the stallion had killed Baskoulos by a sudden, savage kick? Had it happened while Sibyl was still there?

He approached the mansion. The front door stood wide

open. Light poured onto the wide porch. Servants clustered in the hall, but he could not see Rina, or Shep, or Sibyl.

Headlights bored through the dusk from the direction of the south barn. Emory and the limousine? Or the troopers? He crouched behind a clump of flowering shrubbery; it had a cloying fragrance.

The car raced past. The limousine. It stopped in front of the mansion.

He crossed the driveway, made for the white fence bordering the blacktop. Another car turned into the Plantation from the blacktop, pinned him in the glare of its head lamps, braked hard.

"Don! Don!"

Sibyl, flinging open the door of a taxi, beckoning.

He sprinted, piled in beside her as the taillights of the troopers' car, back at the barn, showed the police car was in motion.

Sibyl flung her arms about him. "I've never been so glad to see anyone in all my life."

"The airport," Don panted, "and step on it, driver. We have to catch a plane."

The driver executed a sharp U turn, saying: "I'm gladda see you, too, mister. I never thought I was gonna get paid for them beers you was suppose to buy me at the Grande Luxe."

Don held Sibyl close. "I'll buy you enough to float this cab if you get us to the airport in time."

He listened tensely for the sound of a pursuing siren. There was none.

XXVI

"WE CAN'T go to the airport." Sibyl gripped his wrist. "I have to see Hay-Hay, find out about——"

"Madame Marbola?" His lips were close to her ear; he spoke softly. "I found out about her. At Hay-Hay's motel room. She's dead."

"*Brrr!*" She shuddered. "Another . . . of the Lois things?"

"Same style, same weapon, probably the same stabber."

"Then—if the gypsy's been murdered—how can we learn where Timmy is?"

"Tell you on the plane . . . if we get to the airport without being picked up." He knew very well those troopers had seen the taxi make that fast turnaround in the Old Plantation driveway and speed off toward town. Yet the cop car wasn't pursuing the cab. Only reason could be that they had a two-way, short wave, were calling other cars to converge on the area, set up road blocks. "Driver?"

"Yuh?"

"Sometimes the longest way 'round is the shortest way home. Know what I mean?"

"Don't explain it to me," the driver said over his shoulder. "Let me guess. Then I won't be boxed in if they pick me up after I get you to Bluegrass Field. I know a back way, over toward Cynthiana, cut around, come back in on the Versailles pike. Take a little longer."

"Try it," Don said.

The taxi swooped off onto a dirt road, careened around precarious curves, climbed short, steep hills, plunged down across narrow bridges.

Sibyl said: "This wasn't the cab I called, at all. I'd been frantic to get over to the Motel Grand Luxe because Mister Jefferson insisted the jockey must be there if he wasn't at Keeneland. I didn't believe it, at first, because Charlie Daw had been so explicit that Hay-Hay was at the Old Plantation. So I went after Peter B., who blew his top completely when he found I was from Ambletts. Told me to get the hell off the place. Claimed he didn't know where Hay-Hay was but knew damn well Rina would be with him."

"Where'd you see Baskoulos?"

"In the south barn. He was with a stallion he'd just brought over from Ireland . . . "

"*Politure.* No one else around when you talked to him?"

"Not a soul. Honestly, I thought he was going to beat me up. He came after me; I tell you I *ran*, not walked, to the nearest exit. And went over to the mansion, to the kitchen door. There was an old Negro servant—the butler, I suppose —he let me use the phone to call a cab. And I waited and waited and called again; finally they told me the cab was on its way, would be there in a minute—and I walked out to the highway to meet it—and it was this one. The driver said he'd take me, but first he had to collect a fare from a young feller with white hair—they'd told him at the Grand Luxe you'd come here in the Baskoulos limousine—so of course I made him come back to get you . . . "

"Nice nick-of-timing. They were taking pot shots at me, back there."

"Peter B. was?"

"No." He told her how he had discovered the Greek's corpse, adding: "Troopers didn't know, when they came piling

165

in the barn after me, that Baskoulos was dead. They want me for questioning about that gypsy swindler."

"What chance is there," Sibyl asked fearfully, "that we'll get Timmy back alive—when there have been three of these ghastly murders?"

The driver said: "I'm cuttin' off my roof lights so they don't spot me for a taxi; I ain't supposed to, but it looks like we're gonna make it okay."

"You're my boy." There were no police cars in sight as they reached Bluegrass Field.

The driver looked at the bill Don gave him. "For this I'll even take a lie-detector test. Luck to you both."

"We'll need plenty of it." Don led Sibyl to the waiting room.

The charter pilot was on a stool at the fountain, chatting with the counter girl.

The Grumman was ready to go, the flight plan for the return already filed. In five minutes the motors were being revved. Another three and they had the Go light from Control, were rocketing down the runway.

As they took off, gained altitude, Sibyl pointed to the ground. A red, flashing light moved swiftly in toward the field from the Versailles pike. Police!

Don nodded; it was unnecessary to tell her that the flight plan would be consulted, the Newark Airport alerted, so that when the Grumman was ready to come in for a landing, another police car would be waiting. No good fretting about that, yet.

He did tell her about the call from Edith, the ransom note, the cash in the suitcase, the need to get back to New York in time for her to be at Grand Luxe Commissary #7 by midnight.

She was whipped. "I can't believe that a murderer who would knife two women to death would spare a teen-age boy;

it just doesn't seen possible I'll ever see Timmy alive again."

"Somebody was scheming to gain time," he told her. "Time to put Peter B. out of the way, maybe. Now Rina's free to marry her jockey; she'll inherit some—perhaps all—of the Baskoulos millions; there'll be no question of legitimacy about the child who's on the way. If all that was what the schemer was waiting for, it could be they'll let Timmy live now, let him go." He showed her the black card with the cryptic notation.

"What is it?" she asked.

"An address, I think. Could be the place they're holding Timmy. YM could stand for Yosef Maginn."

Sibyl studied the card. "V, E, T, R, P, E, T . . . it must be in code."

"Gypsy code," he agreed. "Might be a Romanian word. But if you make the midnight contact, we won't have to unravel it."

The plane droned on over the mountains, mist-wreathed peaks not far below. The lights of Charleston, the luminous ribbon of the Kanawha, the clustered glow of small mountain towns.

She told him how she had found herself, on the flight westward, sitting across the aisle from a handsome young woman in a Bahama Sand suit, had decided her plane companion was the gypsy who had taken in Lois Anderson and Frank Wilmar. When she had glimpsed the necklace of gold coins which Timmy had described, she had tried to engage the woman in conversation, but Madame Marbola had not responded. So Sibyl had made up her mind to trail the gypsy if she went on to Lexington.

But as she had descended the steps from the plane at Blue-grass Field, an attendant had loudly paged "Miss Sibyl Forde, Miss Sibyl Forde." Naturally she had not wanted to disclose her identity—if the gypsy had anything to do with Timmy's kidnaping, the name of Forde would put Madame Marbola on her guard. So she had gone right on, ignoring the attendant and his yellow envelope.

Evidently the gypsy had been alarmed anyhow; she had taxied directly to the race track, and while Sibyl had had no difficulty following her there, the woman had given her the slip almost immediately by disappearing into the barn area. Sibyl had searched the barns herself, had made inquiries of exercise boys, jockeys, and grooms but nobody seemed to have noticed the gypsy.

"Then I tried to locate Hay-Hay," Sibyl added wearily, "and finally trailed him to the jockeys' Recreation Room, then lost him again; he'd gone to the steam room. Meantime, I'd called the airport, had Western Union read your wire to me. Then I'd called the store and of course you'd left Ambletts. Finally, after waiting an hour for Hay-Hay to emerge from the steam room—the races had started by then—I gave up and hunted down Charlie Daw. And *he* sent me off to the Old Plantation on that wild-goose chase."

"Maybe it worked out better that way. If you'd stayed close to Madame Marbola, I might have found you in that trunk instead of her." Don pulled her head over onto his shoulder. "You didn't get a wink of sleep last night. Doze off, now; be another couple of hours before we get to Newark."

She fell asleep quickly. He concentrated on the cryptic card. The pilot called back:

"Radio says fog coming in over Newark Bay and the Hackensack. May not amount to anything but doesn't sound too good, right now."

"Play it safe, boy." *You're a fine one to say that! You've been gambling with other people's lives for the last forty-eight hours! You're still gambling with Timmy's!*

The motors roared. The Grumman seemed to be standing still in a sea of mist. Don returned to the black card.

Yosef Maginn, okay. Four T's in a row. Forty? And the
TO . . . how about 42?

42 VETRPET.RD. The RD could stand for Road, couldn't it?
Yosef Maginn, 42 VETRPET Road, TVIL.SI.

Richmond! Timmy had telephoned from a Richmond
number—that was Staten Island. SI.

And TVIL.? Don wasn't acquainted with Staten Island but
he had heard of Tottenville. Yosef Maginn, 42 VETRPET Road,
Tottenville, Staten Island. *Or are you just making it easy for
yourself?* Anyhow, what is that VETRPET?

"No ceiling at Newark," said the pilot tautly.

"What's the nearest place to New York you can land
safely?"

"Bordentown, maybe. Five hundred feet there."

Eleven-thirty. Bordentown was sixty miles from downtown Manhattan. They'd never make it by midnight.

"Make it Bordentown," said Don bleakly.

XXVII

THERE HAD been no fog when the Grumman had finally touched down at Bordentown, but it had begun to rain; it rained softly, like a woman's hopeless tears, all the way to the Goethals Bridge. And all the way, in the taxicab they had called to the airport, Don sat with an arm around a desperately unhappy Sibyl and kept repeating "VETRPET . . . VETRPET . . ."

Occasionally he would silently interrupt himself to admit that he was beyond his depth. *How come you're swimming against the tide, boy; all you had to do was turn this whole thing over to Dooley, as Bob Stolz had suggested—or even to those tough Kentucky troopers—and you wouldn't be on half a dozen different spots at once.* He had a ready answer—though it did not completely satisfy him: *The Lexington murders aren't your business; your business is to get the boy back home.*

Sibyl said: "Stop long enough for me to call Edith."

He looked at his watch. "Better not. Quarter to one, now. If we give the party who went to Commissary #7 time to get back with word that nobody showed up with the ransom, it might be bad for Timmy. I don't know how long it would take to come from downtown Manhattan to wherever VETRPET—" he turned to face her. "That must be it—a phonetic cipher."

"What?" she began.

"Driver, pull in here! At the gas station, right here." Don cranked down the window on his side as the pump attendant came out. "You familiar with this part of the Island?"

"Lived here in Tottenville seven, eight years now." The pump man tore off a handful of windshield paper.

"Know where Featherbed Road is?"

"Sure. Straight on past the third traffic light, next road on your right." The attendant peered in at Sibyl. "It's not such a much as a residential section—shantytown and trailer camps, like that. We got some real fine places if you're——"

"Not figuring on staying there," Don said. "Just looking for someone, thanks."

The cab sped on down the wet pavement.

"VETRPET," Sibyl murmured. "Why, that's just what it sounds like!"

"Another gypsy would probably have understood it right off." Don took Rina's pistol from his pocket. "Can't tell what we'll run into." He gave her the gun.

At the third traffic light, the cab cut right. "What number, mister?"

"Just keep rolling." Don sized up the unpainted shacks, the shanties patched with rusty sheet iron, the lot piled high with junked cars, the trailers with makeshift awnings, the muddy attempts at flower gardens.

"There!" Sibyl exclaimed. "The Caddy clan!"

At the left were half a dozen huge, new shiny aluminum trailers—ten wide, forty to fifty long. Beside each was a big car—Lincolns, Buicks, an ancient Pierce Arrow, one all-black antiquated chariot, a Cadillac. There were lights in four of the trailers.

"This where you wanna stop?" The driver slowed.

"Keep going." Don saw only one building near the new

171

trailers—a metal garage, behind one of the unlighted trailers.

A head appeared at a lighted window, a head bound in a bright yellow scarf.

"Whaddya know!" the driver muttered. "Gyppos. Jeeze, how you figure they can afford mobile homes like them?"

"Not by reading tea leaves," Don said. "Turn right here, stop at the next block."

The waters of the Kill glittered like hammered pewter in the distance, as Don helped Sibyl out of the cab. "If we're not back in half an hour, drive around to the station house, tell the law we were last seen on Featherbed Road among the gyppos."

"If they's gonna be a brawl," the driver leaned down, came up with a jack handle, "I'm a good man with this."

"Bet you would be," Don agreed. "But this is one deal we have to play out on our own. However, if you can spare a flashlight . . . ?"

The driver could and did.

Don led Sibyl back to the VETRPET. "Hate to march you cross-country but we can't stay on the road."

Sibyl said: "I'll wade through an alligator pool if Timmy's at the other end."

They slogged through saw grass that slashed at their ankles and tore their clothing, through muddy morasses, stumbled over ash piles and deposits of tin cans and old bedsprings.

"One good thing," Don muttered, "they don't keep dogs, nowadays."

Sibyl wiped rain off her face with her sleeve. "Why would that one have a garage? None of the others have; they just leave their cars out in the weather."

"It's one of those portable, put-it-up-yourself things. It could have been set up in half a day." He held her arm. "Don't trip over any tin cans now . . . bring the whole clan down on us."

They crept up behind the garage, moved cautiously around the side: through the rainy darkness came the wild melody of a violin, a czardas . . .

The doors of the garage were padlocked; the padlock was big and brassy; it was fitted through a strong hasp.

"They'd never keep Timmy locked up in that," Sibyl whispered. "There's no ventilation."

Don put his ear to the metal door.

Faintly, in an off-key, sing-songy falsetto, the tune came through the strains of the faraway violin:

". . . *an' on this little branch, there was a little twig . . .*"

He motioned to Sibyl to listen:

". . . *prettiest little twig that yever did see*
Twig on the branch, branch on the limb, limb on the tree
An' the green grass grew all around, all around——"

"TIMMY!" she cried out in her excitement, pounding on the door.

The falsetto stopped.

"Easy," Don cautioned.

She rapped quickly on the metal: "*Shave-and-a-haircut, bay-rum.*"

"Hey!" The boy was wary. "Who's that? *Aunt Sib?*"

"Oh, Timmy! Timmy! We'll have you out in a minute!"

"Not going to be that simple." Don considered shooting the hasp off, realized there'd be too great a danger to the boy. Yet, short of a hacksaw, he could think of no way to get that padlock off.

Headlights probed the darkness; a car came splashing down Featherbed Road. A big car . . .

"Stay here," Don told Sibyl. "Pretend to be trying a key in the padlock." He flung himself on the wet ground, crawled around the side of the garage as the lights curved in past the trailer, pointed at the garage.

173

Instinctively Sibyl turned, then remembered, bent over the padlock.

The Cadillac stopped, motor running, lights on. A muscular figure leaped out, ran at Sibyl, caught her by the shoulder, flung her back.

Then Don was on him, clubbing him with the barrel of the gun, pinning Yosef Maginn's shoulders into the dirt.

"Key, Sib . . . get the key. Must have it on him."

She found it quickly, in his trouser pocket, whirled to fit it in the padlock.

Don had his hands full; the gypsy fought like a crazy ram, butting and kicking. Don clubbed him again across the temple. And heard Timmy's agonized cry:

"Don't, don't, Mister Cadee. Don't hurt him. He saved my life. He kept them from killing me."

XXVIII

THE SHINY new trailers erupted in wild outcries and a horde of gypsies—men, women and children, converging on Don and his prisoner.

Don yanked Yosef to his feet, prodded him with the shiny new pistol:

"Tell your friends to keep hands off or you'll get hurt. Tell 'em, quick!"

Yosef shouted orders in some language foreign to Don, submitted meekly to being marched into the garage, his twenty-five-dollar Ambletts' silk shirt glistening with rain and sweat.

Don noticed the strong fingers, the grimy nails. *Were these the hands which had tightened the noose about his neck at Forest Hills?*

Sibyl clung to Timmy; the boy wept with relief, punctuating his sniffles with appeals for clemency:

"Joe really did save me, Aunt Sib . . . he hid me in here while they were hunting for me . . . I was really sort of guarding the merchandise, see?"

Don saw; stacked green and lavender boxes from the Store Superlative, red and white striped wrappings from a famous Thirty-second Street store—the garage was a storehouse of stolen goods, in the original packages.

175

Sibyl held Rina's gun at a tentative angle. "Are we going to have to shoot our way out of here, Don?"

"No." He saw one of the gypsy men getting into Yosef's car, wondered if the fellow was going to plow straight ahead into the garage. "We're going to sit tight and wait for the Tottenville cops." The gypsy cut the motor but left the lights of the Cadillac on.

Timmy said: "Are you going to have Joe arrested?"

One of the gamins hurled a pop bottle; it missed Sibyl by inches. Don waggled his pistol in warning. "We can't let him go, Timmy. But if he feels like telling us who worked with him on this business, we'll go easy on him."

Yosef spat scornfully. "You think I talk?"

"I suppose you will have to be punished, Joe," Timmy said judiciously, "but if you'll play ball with Mister Cadee I bet you won't have to spend very much time in prison."

Yosef said nothing, but he made pacifying gestures toward the menacing members of his clan.

Don observed the pile of sports jackets which had evidently been fixed for the boy to sleep on, noticed a small collection of empty milk bottles and discarded candy bar wrappings. Timmy hadn't been mistreated; that gave Yosef Maginn a gold star in Don's book.

"You're thinking that you'll get your wife in trouble if you talk," he said to the gypsy.

"Mary is my sister, not my wife."

"She was your sister," Don said. "She was killed down in Lexington, Kentucky, yesterday afternoon. Person who stuck a knife in her back must have been afraid your sister would speak out of turn. Might be better for you if you speak out now."

Yosef glared; veins in his forehead swelled; he held out a clenched fist. "You lie."

"Why should I?" Don asked evenly. "We have our boy

back; we have the stolen property; we have you. Why should I tell you something that's not true when you'd only find out the facts in a few hours? I saw your sister's corpse in a trunk in a motel room in Lexington less than twelve hours ago."

Sibyl touched the gypsy's arm: "Don't you want to help us catch the killer, Joe?"

Timmy came close to Yosef, looked up at him solemnly. "You don't want to let a murderer get away, do you?"

Yosef breathed hard, stared at the dirt floor of the garage. "It was Baskoulos put us up to it. We stay at Jamaica, last week; Mary had a sucker there, this jockey Greld. He pays her twenty, sometimes twenty-five dollars a day for telling him what horses he should ride. One day, week ago, I'm over there, looking for Mary. I see Baskoulos talking to this Greld and another man, the jockey's agent. When he finishes with them he sees me and says 'Haven't I seen you around our commissary in New York?' and I tell him sure, I work for him, coppersmith work, so how about putting me wise to a good thing the next day? He thinks it over and says maybe he could give us something pretty good at that but he would have to see me later. And he asks me where he can find me; I tell him where our trailer is parked."

An enormously fat old woman in a green head scarf and a turkey-red skirt rushed at Don, caught his coat, screaming insults.

Yosef drove her off. "Stay out of this, Mamma! I do what I have to do. Leave me alone!" He went on: "Baskoulos comes to our trailer, meets Mary and makes us a proposition—we can clean up better than on any bet at the fifty-dollar windows. We are to help him get something on his wife; he wants to divorce her; he thinks she has been too friendly with this jockey who is paying Mary the big, fat fee every day. He will give us five thousand dollars if Mary can get something on Missus Baskoulos that he can use in court."

Don asked: "Was it his idea to have the scare session down on Harkover Street? With the chemical on the jug cork to clear the 'muddy' water and the other chemical to make the smoke red and the gimmicked microphone to make the flame shriek?"

"Him and Mary worked it out together," Yosef said glumly. "She'd done all that magic stuff before, but he thought it would put the fear of God into Missus Baskoulos."

Don said: "Whose idea was it to get her to bring all the cash she could lay her hands on, to pull the old switcheroo?"

"My sister's. She didn't tell Baskoulos about that, or me either, at first. All she was suppose to do was frighten Missus Baskoulos into making a confession, but she thought there wasn't any reason she couldn't make a few extra bucks by the old *bajour* switch. So she asked Baskoulos could he get a duplicate of his wife's handbag—it would help her to exchange handbags for a minute and maybe read any love letters Missus Baskoulos might have in the bag."

Sibyl nodded. "Then when all your sister found was a bunch of credit coins, she couldn't resist taking those—and cashing in on them, too."

Yosef glowered: "We didn't get paid off, like he promised; he said he had to have something that would be evidence in court and what Mary had learned wasn't good enough. So Mary got mad and decided to hit the stores for enough to get us the five thousand anyway."

Shouts of alarm rose from the clustering gypsies; they scattered into the darkness as the flashing red light of a police car showed, far up Featherbed Road, the roof lights of the taxicab trailing it.

Sibyl asked: "But if Mister Baskoulos didn't know you were going to swindle all this merchandise, why would he have killed our salesgirl when all she wanted was to recover the goods?"

Yosef grunted, held out his hands. "About the Anderson girl, we do not know. It was her murder that made us afraid to do as Baskoulos told us to—he was crazy mad when he find out about the stealing from the store—he wanted us to kill the boy here when we caught him at our trailer in Jamaica . . . "

Timmy ran to Don, seized his arm. "Don't you believe him, Mister Cadee, don't you?"

"No," Don said. "I don't believe it . . . but I'm beginning to understand it, Timmy."

Then the cops were swarming in.

XXIX

BY THE time Yosef had been taken into official custody and the padlock had been replaced on the cache of stolen menswear, it was two-thirty. It took another hour for the booking at the Tottenville police station and the questioning by the uniformed officers. What with Sibyl calling her sister-in-law and Timmy's choked-up conversation with his mother and the boy's fervent farewell to his gypsy "guardian"—it was four o'clock before the cab driver got his bonus: the long haul to Manhattan via the ferry and on to Edith's.

Don didn't make the trip to Forest Hills. The boy was safe, but there was still a spot of unfinished business for a Protection Chief who felt a responsibility to store employees. So he dropped off at Ambletts, lugged the new suitcase with its burden of old bills up to his Third floor office.

There were a dozen Urgent memos on his desk; he discarded all but one: the typed list of telephone numbers of the tenants on the eighth, ninth, tenth and eleventh floors of the Mid-Broad Building.

Big Pat had written at the bottom of the list:

> There's only this one I have checked that has the two sevens and the naught. I would have gone to case the joint myself but I thought I would not rush in where angels might wish to tread: I don't expect to be an angel for some time yet.

It took Don half an hour to convince Homicide that the Bureau should rouse its hard-working captain at half past five, but Dooley eventually called back.

"You know there's an arrest order out for you, Cadee?"

"Lexington?"

"I warned the boys down in Kentucky to be on the lookout for Mary Maginn so they returned the favor by tipping me off that you're wanted for leaving the scene of a crime, concealing information about a homicide, evading arrest, and half a dozen other charges."

"Is that all they told you, Captain?"

"No. They said Peter Baskoulos had been accidentally stomped to death by a prize stallion, that his wife was under the care of her physician at the Old Plantation, and that Hay-Hay Greld was out on bond after being hauled in on suspicion of murdering his old pal, Mary Maginn."

Don said: "I can give you better news than that."

"Such as. . . ?"

"The Forde kid is home, safe and sound. The merchandise that was rooked out of our store has been found. We have Mary Maginn's brother over in the hoosegow on Staten Island. He's made a free and full confession."

Dooley grumbled: "Why don't you give up that store job and go to work for the force, Cadee! Maybe then——"

"Wait. The free and full confession leaves something to be desired. I might be able to satisfy that desire if you'll meet me in front of the Mid-Broad Building in, say—half an hour."

"You got yourself a date."

"If you get there before I do, borrow a passkey from the night-side man, Captain."

Don took ten to shave. The touch of the blade on his throat was sharp-edged torture. The mirror told him he was considerably the worse for wear. But, he told his reflection, he was considerably luckier than some of the other acquaintances of the Merchant of Murder had been.

He walked over to Broadway and turned uptown. He wanted the walk; he'd had enough of taxicabs. Nor did he bother to buy a newspaper; he'd come too close to being a headline, himself.

Dooley was waiting for him with the passkey. In the Up car the Captain said: "That elevator operator who gave us the description of Peter Baskoulos sort of reneged on his identification when we showed him a photograph of the big restaurant boy, Cadee."

"Did you check out on his alibi at the Racquet and Mallet?"

"We did. Doorman couldn't recall the Greek's having been near the club Wednesday afternoon."

"Ten," said the night operator.

They walked along the corridor.

"Ten-seventeen," Don said quietly. "The one where the light is still on."

Dooley quirked an eyebrow. "Importers?" he muttered. "What do they import?"

"Race horses. Better get set for action, Captain."

Dooley used the passkey, opened the door gently.

The tall man behind the flat-top desk came to his feet swiftly; he wore a suit of shaggy Donegal tweed and an expression of consternation.

"Captain Dooley," Don said, "meet Sheppard Jefferson, manager of stables for the late Peter Baskoulos, whose name he used on occasion, to mystify his gypsy friends."

Shep Jefferson's attempt at a jovial smile was not a success. He clapped one hand against his long, narrow face in the leaning-against-a-tree attitude, reached for his coat pocket with the other.

"Better search him carefully," Don said. "He may not have a gun but he likes to carry a knife . . . sort vets use to operate

on horses. Also, he's right handy with a strangler's noose—
look out!"

But Dooley had fired before the manager of the Old
Plantation had his hand quite out of his pocket.

The hand held no pistol when he withdrew it as he staggered
against a file cabinet. Not even a thin, sharp blade.

Only a small, blue-black pill.

XXX

"YOU MEAN"—Sibyl stood in front of the medicine-cabinet mirror in the Protection Office, primping, with that cat-lapping-thick-cream air of a girl well aware she doesn't need to primp—"that Yosef made up that tale about being hired by Peter the B.?"

"Not at all." Don let her see that he appreciated her. "As Wally would say, it was a mistake in identity on Yosef's part. He'd worked as an occasional pot mender at the Grand Luxe Commissary but he'd never seen Baskoulos there. Yosef had seen Shep Jefferson with Baskoulos' jockey, may have heard 'Mister Baskoulos' mentioned by Hay-Hay, and jumped to the conclusion that the manager was the boss himself. Shep Jefferson thought he saw a chance to turn the gypsy's mistake to his own advantage; simply kept up the pretense."

"Madame Marbola didn't catch on—that Jefferson was masquerading as the millionaire?"

"Of course she knew. Probably she never let on to Yosef that she did; I don't think she had much respect for her brother's intelligence. But Mary must have known, otherwise there'd have been no need to rig up that confirmation-of-the-customer call from Menswear to the EssJay number, the Ca 7-0791 that Lois finally recalled. Mary had arranged that in advance; she knew Mitzi Lepreaux would be there to carry out the fraud."

"Mitzi? The French maid you lent your suite to?"

"Rina's maid. She'd been playing around with Shep Jefferson for a long time, acting as his pipe line for inside information on the domestic situation in the Baskoulos family —and out of it. She went to the EssJay office that day especially to be there when Mary, as Missus B., called in to speak to 'Peter.' "

"EssJay. His initials."

"Sure; I ought to have spotted it long before Pat dug up those phone numbers for me."

"What on earth was he doing in that hole-in-the-wall office when he was supposed to be managing a million-dollar string of race horses, Don?"

"Putting over fast ones . . . and not on the track. Making deals with Irish breeders to sell imported thoroughbreds to Baskoulos at double their value and pocketing the difference through his own company. But he was afraid the Greek was getting wise; he didn't like the idea of his little graft—it wasn't so little at that—coming to an end. So when he heard from Mitzi about Rina's affair with Hay-Hay Greld, Shep thought he saw a chance to parlay a death in the family into control of the Old Plantation. If Baskoulos should somehow come to a violent end, Hay-Hay could marry Rina, the manager who'd done so much to help the harassed wife would be in like Flynn with the widow and her second husband. A nice snug scheme."

"It ganged a-gley . . . "

"Because everybody in it was too greedy, Sib. In order to get a lock on Rina, Shep thought he had to have something on her. First, he thought it would be an admission that Hay-Hay was the father of the oncoming infant. Later, he figured that Rina's remark—recorded on that wire which damn near cost me my neck—about 'taking matters into her own hands' might be held over her as a sort of announcement that she

185

had meant to murder her husband. That's why he was so desperate to get his hands on the recording."

"That makes sense." Sibyl came to perch on the corner of his desk. "But why kill poor Lois? That was senseless."

"He panicked when he saw her walk into his office and gape at the box of menswear items on his desk."

"Mary gave some of the stuff to *him?*"

"A peace offering. Dooley got this out of him while they were riding over to the Detention Ward in the ambulance. Seems Shep went to the Maginn trailer over by the Jamaica race track Tuesday night, the night Timmy went prowling around over there looking for the Caddy clan at Steve Liebman's suggestion. He found out Yosef had caught your nephew; that made him afraid that somehow we'd trace the stolen merchandise to the Maginns. To pacify him, Mary promised to move to Tottenville that same night. She said they'd store the stuff where nobody could find it. And she gave him a couple hundred dollors' worth of the swindle's proceeds. He took them back to the EssJay office; they were still on his desk in plain sight when Lois walked in on him."

"She grabbed a pair of shorts, to have as evidence——"

"——and he made a grab for her. She fled. He chased her. By some freak of coincidence, no one saw her running or heard him going pellmell after her. On the staircase he caught up with her, used that damn veterinarian's knife."

"You said everyone in the scheme was too greedy. Yosef wasn't——"

"No. Ol' Joe's too soft-hearted to be greedy; besides he likes kids, most gypsies do. But Mary liked nothing except money. She got thirty thousand from Rina, but that didn't satisfy her. She kept right on, even after she'd learned about Lois's death, knowing who had killed her. She wrote that ransom note to see if she could drain another five thousand out of Timmy's folks—she'd already kept the five thousand

Shep Jefferson paid her to stage that scare séance—and then she had to streak down to Kentucky to see what final drop of blood she might squeeze out of Hay-Hay Greld, or maybe by blackmailing Rina. I've no doubt at all she did try to put the B on Jefferson and that he killed her to shut her up once and for all."

"Why did she send that 'Merchant of Murder' warning to Hay-Hay?"

"Oh, to impress him with her powers of prophecy. She'd foreseen—and no crystal ball needed—that Jefferson was going to murder Baskoulos—none of the manager's preparations would have been necessary unless there was a coffin at the end of the road—and she thought that Hay-Hay would believe in her more strongly than ever if he thought she'd called that turn ahead of the event."

"You're the one that had second sight."

"No. Mine is all *post factum*. But better *l* than *n*."

"Give me your *post factum* opinion on why Charlie Daw sent me will-o'-the-wisping over to the horse farm when he knew Hay-Hay wouldn't be there."

"Mere attempt to avoid more *femme* trouble. All Charlie Daw's woes were women-woes. Rina, Madame Marbola—and then a redhead with fire in her eyes. He just meant to sidetrack you, get you out of his way."

"Speaking of which, why didn't Shep Jefferson stay down in Kentucky where he'd be out of your way, *maestro*?"

"He thought the bigger risk would be to leave traces of his ownership of EssJay, maybe also some of the loot from Ambletts, where I might run it to earth. So he told Dooley."

"According to Timmy, Shep Jeff was right; my brash nephew thinks you could find the grain of sand on the beach, the needle in the haystack——"

"How is he?"

"Just about now," she glanced at the desk clock, "he's reporting to the Stock Room. By the way, he says to tell you he isn't going to claim any of the reward; he thinks it all ought to go to Lois's mother."

"*That's* my boy." He smiled wearily. "How about your reward; you're entitled to one, after shagging all over creation in cabs and planes and——"

"Exactly what," she inquired, "did you have in mind?"

The smile broadened. "How about a real deep-dish week end at the newly acquired Cadee Cottage for Old Protection People up in the wilds of Connecticut?"

"Hm . . . fishing for lake trout . . . with me at the oars."

"Strolling through cathedral pines . . . "

"Basking in the sun . . . "

"Lounging before the open fire——"

"And me," she finished, "doing the cooking. You know, I'll love every minute of it."